The Spectre Bride

with *Auriol and A Night in Rome*

by

William Harrison Ainsworth

Contents

The Spectre Bride

The castle of Hernswolf, at the close of the year 1655, was the resort of fashion and gaiety. The baron of that name was the most powerful nobleman in Germany, and equally celebrated for the patriotic achievements of his sons, and the beauty of his only daughter. The estate of Hernswolf, which was situated in the centre of the Black Forest, had been given to one of his ancestors by the gratitude of the nation, and descended with other hereditary possessions to the family of the present owner. It was a castellated, gothic mansion, built according to the fashion of the times, in the grandest style of architecture, and consisted principally of dark winding corridors, and vaulted tapestry rooms, magnificent indeed in their size, but ill-suited to private comfort, from the very circumstance of their dreary magnitude. A dark grove of pine and mountain ash encompassed the castle on every side, and threw an aspect of gloom around the scene, which was seldom enlivened by the cheering sunshine of heaven.

*　　*　　*　　*　　*

The castle bells rung out a merry peal at the approach of a winter twilight, and the warder was stationed with his retinue on the battlements, to announce the arrival of the company who were invited to share the amusements that reigned within the walls. The Lady Clotilda, the baron's only daughter, had but just attained her seventeenth year, and a brilliant assembly was invited to celebrate the birthday. The large vaulted apartments were thrown open for the reception of the numerous guests, and the gaieties of the evening had scarcely commenced when the clock from the dungeon tower was beard to strike with unusual solemnity, and on the instant a tall stranger, arrayed in a deep suit of black, made his appearance in the ballroom. He bowed courteously on every side, but was received by all with the strictest reserve. No one knew who he was or whence he came, but it was evident from his appearance, that he was a nobleman of the first rank, and though his introduction was accepted with distrust, he was treated by all with respect. He addressed himself particularly to the daughter of the baron, and was so intelligent in his remarks, so lively in his sallies, and so fascinating in his address, that he quickly interested the feelings of his young and sensitive auditor. In fine, after some hesitation on the part of the host, who, with the rest of the company, was unable to approach the stranger with indifference, he was requested to remain a few days at the castle, an invitation which was cheerfully accepted.

The dead of the night drew on, and when all had retired to rest, the dull heavy bell was heard swinging to and fro in the grey tower, though there was scarcely a breath to move the forest trees. Many of the guests, when they met the next morning at the breakfast table, averred that there had been sounds as of the most heavenly music, while all persisted in affirming that they had heard awful noises, proceeding, as it seemed, from the apartment which the stranger at that time occupied. He soon, however, made his appearance at the breakfast circle, and when the circumstances of the preceding night were alluded to, a dark smile of unutterable meaning played round his saturnine features. and then relapsed into an expression of the deepest melancholy. He addressed his conversation principally to Clotilda, and when he talked of the different climes he had visited, of the sunny regions of Italy, where the very air breathes the fragrance of flowers, and the summer breeze sighs over a land of sweets; when he spoke to her of those delicious countries, where the smile of the day sinks into the softer beauty of the night, and the loveliness of heaven is never for an instant obscured, he drew tears of regret from the bosom of his fair auditor, and for the first time she regretted that she was yet at home

Days rolled on, and every moment increased the fervour of the inexpressible sentiments with which the stranger had inspired her. He never discoursed of love, but he looked it in his language, in his manner, in the insinuating tones of his voice, and in the slumbering softness of his smile, and when he found that he had succeeded in inspiring, her with favourable sentiments, a sneer of the most diabolical meaning spoke for an instant, and died again on his dark featured countenance. When he met her in the company of her parents, he was at once respectful and submissive, and it was only when alone with her, in her ramble through the dark recesses of the forest, that he assumed the guise of the more impassioned admirer.

As he was sitting one evening with the baron in the wainscoted apartment of the library, the conversation happened to turn upon supernatural agency. The stranger remained reserved and mysterious during the discussion, but when the baron in a jocular manner denied the existence of spirits, and satirically mocked their appearance, his eyes glowed with unearthly lustre, and his form seemed to dilate to more than its natural dimensions. When the conversation had ceased, a fearful pause of a few seconds and a chorus of celestial harmony was heard pealing through the dark forest glade. All were entranced with delight, but the stranger was disturbed and gloomy; he looked at his noble host with compassion, and something like a tear swam in his dark eye. After the lapse of a few seconds, the music died gently in the distance, and all was hushed as before. The baron soon after quitted the apartment, and was followed almost immediately by the stranger. He had not long been absent, when an awful noise, as of a person in the agonies of death, was heard, and the Baron was discovered stretched dead along the corridors. His countenance was convulsed with pain, and the grip of a human hand was visible on his blackened throat. The alarm was instantly given, the castle searched in every direction, but the stranger was seen no more. The body of the baron, in the meantime, was quietly committed to the earth, and the remembrance of the dreadful transaction, recalled but as a thing that once was.

*   *   *   *   *

After the departure of the stranger, who had indeed fascinated her very senses, the spirits of the gentle Clotilda evidently declined. She loved to walk early and late in the walks that he had once frequented, to recall his last words; to dwell on his sweet smile; and wander to the spot where she had once discoursed with him of love. She avoided all society, and never seemed to he happy but when left alone in the solitude of her chamber. It was then that she gave vent to her affliction in tears; and the love that the pride of maiden modesty concealed in public, burst forth in the hours of privacy. So beauteous, yet so resigned was the fair mourner, that she seemed already an angel freed from the trammels of the world, and prepared to take her flight to heaven.

As she was one summer evening rambling to the sequestered spot that had been selected as her favourite residence, a slow step advanced towards her. She turned round, and to her infinite surprise discovered the stranger. He stepped gaily to her side, and commenced an animated conversation. 'You left me,' exclaimed the delighted girl; 'and I thought all happiness was fled from me for ever; but you return, and shall we not again he happy?' – 'Happy,' replied the stranger, with a scornful burst of derision, 'Can I ever he happy again – can there ; – but excuse the agitation my love, and impute it to the pleasure I experience at our meeting. Oh! I have many things to tell you; aye! and many kind words to receive; is it not so, sweet one? Come, tell me truly, have you been happy in my absence? No! I see in that sunken eye, in that pallid cheek, that the poor wanderer has at least gained some slight interest in the heart of his beloved. I have roamed to other climes, I have seen other nations; I have met with other females, beautiful and accomplished, but I have met with but one angel, and she is here before me. Accept this simple offering of my affection, dearest,' continued the stranger, plucking a heath-rose from its stem; 'it is beautiful as the wild flowers that deck thy hair, and sweet as is the love I bear thee.' – 'It is sweet, indeed,' replied Clotilda, 'but its sweetness must wither ere night closes around. It is beautiful, but its beauty is short-lived, as the love evinced by man. Let not this, then, be the type of thy attachment; bring me the delicate evergreen, the sweet flower that blossoms throughout the year, and I will say, as I wreathe it in my hair, "The violets have bloomed and died – the roses have flourished and decayed; but the evergreen is still young, and so is the love of heart!" – you will not – cannot desert me. I live but in you; you are my hopes, my thoughts, my existence itself : and if I lose you, I lose my all – I was but a solitary wild flower in the wilderness of nature, until you transplanted me to a more genial soil; and can you now break the fond heart you first taught to glow with passion?' – 'Speak not thus,' returned the stranger, 'it rends my very soul to hear you; leave me – forget me – avoid me for ever – or your eternal ruin must ensue. I am a thing abandoned of God and man – and did you but see the scared heart that scarcely beats within this moving mass of deformity, you would flee me, as you would an adder in your path. Here is my heart, love, feel how cold it is; there is no pulse that betrays its emotion; for all is chilled and dead as the friends I once knew.' – 'You are unhappy, love, and your poor Clotilda shall stay to succour you. Think not I can abandon you in your misfortunes. No! I will wander with thee through the wide world, and be thy servant, thy slave, if thou wilt have it so. I will shield thee from the night winds, that they blow not too roughly on thy unprotected head. I will defend thee from the tempest that howls around; and though the cold world may devote thy name to scorn – though friends may fall off, and associates wither in the grave, there shall he one fond heart who shall love thee better in thy misfortune, and cherish thee, bless thee still.' She ceased, and her blue eyes swam in tears, as she turned it glistening with affection towards the stranger. He averted his head from her gaze, and a scornful sneer of the darkest, the deadliest malice passed over, his fine countenance. In an instant, the expression subsided; his fixed glassy eye resumed its unearthly chillness, and he turned once again to his companion. 'It is the hour of sunset,' he exclaimed; 'the soft, the beauteous hour, when the hearts of lovers are happy, and nature smiles in unison with their feelings; but to me it will smile no longer – ere the morrow dawns I shall very far, from the house of my beloved; from the scenes where my heart is enshrined, as in a sepulchre. But must I leave thee, Dearest flower of the wilderness, to be the sport of a whirlwind, the prey of the mountain blast?' – 'No, we will not part,' replied the impassioned girl; *'where thou goest, will I go; thy home shall be my home; and thy God shall be my God.'* – 'Swear it, swear it,' resumed the stranger, wildly grasping her by the hand; 'swear to the fearful oath I shall dictate.' He then desired her to kneel, and holding his right hand in a menacing attitude towards heaven, and throwing back his dark raven locks, exclaimed in a strain of bitter imprecation with the ghastly smile of an incarnate fiend, 'May the curses of an offended God,' he cried, 'haunt thee, cling to thee for ever in the tempest and in the calm, in the day and in the night, in sickness and in sorrow, in life and in death, shouldst thou swerve from the promise thou hast here made to be mine. May the dark spirits of the damned howl in thine ears the accursed chorus of fiends – may the air rack thy bosom with the quenchless flames of hell! May thy soul be as the lazar-house of corruption, where the ghost of departed pleasure sits enshrined, as in a grave: where the hundred-headed worm never dies where the fire is never extinguished. May a spirit of evil lord it over thy brow, and proclaim, as thou passest by, "THIS IS THE ABANDONED OF GOD AND MAN;" may fearful spectres haunt thee in the night season; may thy dearest friends drop day by day into the grave, and curse thee with their dying breath: may all that is most horrible in human nature, more solemn than language can frame, or lips can utter, may this, and more than this, be thy eternal portion, shouldst thou violate the oath that thou has taken.' He ceased – hardly knowing what she did, the terrified girl acceded to the awful adjuration, and promised eternal fidelity to him who was henceforth to be her lord. 'Spirits of the damned, I thank thee for thine assistance,' shouted the stranger; 'I have wooed my fair bride bravely. She is mine – mine for ever. – Aye, body and soul both mine; mine in life, and mine in death. What in tears my sweet one, ere yet the honeymoon is past? Why! indeed thou hast cause for weeping: but when next we meet we shall meet to sign the nuptial bond.' He then imprinted a cold salute on the cheek of his young bride, and softening down the unutterable horrors of his countenance, requested her to meet him at eight o'clock on the ensuing evening in the chapel adjoining to the castle of Hernswolf. She turned round to him with a burning sigh, as if to implore protection from himself, but the stranger was gone.

On entering the castle, she was observed to be impressed with deepest melancholy. Her relations vainly endeavoured to ascertain the cause of her uneasiness; but the tremendous oath she had sworn completely paralysed her faculties, and she was fearful of betraying herself by even the slightest intonation of her voice, or the least variable expression of her countenance. When the evening was concluded, the family retired to rest; but Clotilda, who was unable to take repose, from the restlessness of her disposition, requested to remain alone in the library that adjoined her apartment.

All was now deep midnight; every domestic had long since retired to rest, and the only sound that could be distinguished was the sullen howl of the ban-dog as he bayed, the waning moon Clotilda remained in the library in an attitude of deep meditation. The lamp that burnt on the table, where she sat, was dying away, and the lower end of the apartment was already more than half obscured. The clock from the northern angle of the castle tolled out the hour of twelve, and the sound echoed dismally in the solemn stillness of the night. Sudden the oaken door at the farther end of the room was gently lifted on its latch, and a bloodless figure, apparelled in the habiliments of the grave, advanced slowly up the apartment. No sound heralded its approach, as it moved with noiseless steps to the table where the lady was stationed. She did not at first perceive it, till she felt a death-cold hand fast grasped in her own, and heard a solemn voice whisper in her ear, 'Clotilda.' She looked up, a dark figure was standing beside her; she endeavoured to scream, but her voice was unequal to the exertion; her eye was fixed, as if by magic, on the form which, slowly removed the garb that concealed its countenance, and disclosed the livid eyes and skeleton shape of her father. It, seemed to gaze on her with pity, an regret, and mournfully exclaimed – 'Clotilda, the dresses and the servants are ready, the church bell has tolled, and the priest is at the altar, but where is the affianced bride? There is room for her in the grave, and tomorrow shall she be with me.' –

'Tomorrow?' faltered out the distracted girl; 'the spirits of hell shall have registered it, and tomorrow must the bond be cancelled.' The figure ceased – slowly retired, and was soon lost in the obscurity of distance.

The morning – evening – arrived; and already as the hall clock struck eight, Clotilda was on her road to the chapel. It was a dark, gloomy night, thick masses of dun clouds sailed across the firmament, and the roar of the winter wind echoed awfully through the forest trees. She reached the appointed place; a figure was in waiting for her – it advanced – and discovered the features of the stranger. 'Why! this is well, my bride,' he exclaimed, with a sneer; 'and well will I repay thy fondness. Follow me.' They proceeded together in silence through the winding avenues of the chapel, until they reached the adjoining cemetery. Here they paused for an instant; and the stranger, in a softened tone, said, 'But one hour more, and the struggle will be over. And yet this heart of incarnate malice can feel, when it devotes so young, so pure a spirit to the grave. But it must – it must be,' he proceeded, as the memory of her past love rushed on her mind; 'for the fiend whom I obey has so willed it. Poor girl, I am leading thee indeed to our nuptials; but the priest will be death, thy parents the mouldering skeletons that rot in heaps around; and the witnesses our union, the lazy worms that revel on the carious bones of the dead. Come, my young bride, the priest is impatient for his victim.' As they proceeded, a dim blue light moved swiftly before them, and displayed at the extremity of the churchyard the portals of a vault. It was open, and they entered it in silence. The hollow wind came rushing through the

gloomy abode of the dead; and on every side were piled the mouldering remnants of coffins, which dropped piece by piece upon the damp
ml. Every step they took was on a dead body; and the bleached bones
rattled horribly beneath their feet. In the centre of the vault rose a heap
of unburied skeletons, whereon was seated, a figure too awful even for
the darkest imagination to conceive. As they approached it, the hollow
vault rung with a hellish peal of laughter; and every mouldering corpse
seemed endued with unholy life. The stranger paused, and as he
grasped his victim in his hand, one sigh burst from his heart – one tear
glistened in his eye. It was but for an instant; the figure frowned awfully at his vacillation, and waved his gaunt hand.

The stranger advanced; he made certain mystic circles in the air,
uttered unearthly words, and paused in excess of terror. On a sudden
he raised his voice and wildly exclaimed – 'Spouse of the spirit of
darkness, a few moments are yet thine; that thou may'st know to whom
thou hast consigned thyself. I am the undying spirit of the wretch who
curst his Saviour on the cross. He looked at me in the closing hour of
his existence, and that look hath not yet passed away, for I am curst
above all on earth. I am eternally condemned to hell and I must cater
for my master's taste till the world is parched as is a scroll, and the
heavens and the earth have passed away. I am he of whom thou may'st
have read, and of whose feats thou may'st have heard. A million souls
has my master condemned me to ensnare, and then my penance is accomplished, and I may know the repose of the grave. Thou art the
thousandth soul that I have damned. I saw thee in thine hour of purity,
and I marked thee at once for my home. Thy father did I murder for
his temerity, and permitted to warn thee of thy fate; and myself have I
beguiled for thy simplicity. Ha! the spell works bravely, and thou shall
soon see, my sweet one, to whom thou hast linked thine undying for-
tunes, for as long as the seasons shall move on their course of nature –
as long as the lightning shall flash, and the thunders- roll, thy penance
shall be eternal. Look below I and see to what thou art destined.' She
looked, the vault split in a thousand different directions; the earth
yawned asunder; and the roar of mighty waters was heard. A living
ocean of molten fire glowed in the abyss beneath her, and blending
with the shrieks of the damned, and the triumphant shouts of the
fiends, rendered horror more horrible than imagination. Ten millions
of souls were writhing in the fiery flames, and as the boiling billows
dashed them against the blackened rocks of adamant, they cursed with

the blasphemies of despair; and each curse echoed in thunder cross the wave. The stranger rushed towards his victim. For an instant he held her over the burning vista, looked fondly in her face and wept as he were a child. This was but the impulse of a moment; again he grasped her in his arms, dashed her from him with fury; and as her last parting glance was cast in kindness on his face, shouted aloud, 'not mine is the crime, but the religion that thou professest; for is it not said that there is a fire of eternity prepared for the souls of the wicked; and hast not thou incurred its torments?' She, poor girl, heard not, heeded not the shouts of the blasphemer. Her delicate form bounded from rock to rock, over billow, and over foam; as she fell, the ocean lashed itself as it were in triumph to receive her soul, and as she sunk deep in the burning pit, ten thousand voices reverberated from the bottomless abyss, 'Spirit of evil! here indeed is an eternity of torments prepared for thee; for here the worm never dies, and the fire is never quenched.'

Auriol, or The Elixir of Life

Prologue – 1599: Doctor Lamb

The Sixteenth Century drew to a close. It was the last day of the last year, and two hours only were wanting to the birth of another year and of another century.

The night was solemn and beautiful. Myriads of stars paved the deep vault of heaven; the crescent moon hung like a silver lamp in the midst of them; a stream of rosy and quivering light issuing from the north traversed the sky, like the tail of some stupendous comet; while from its point of effluence broke forth, ever and anon, coruscations rivalling in splendour and variety of hue the most brilliant discharge of fireworks.

A sharp frost prevailed; but the atmosphere was clear and dry, and neither wind nor snow aggravated the wholesome rigour of the season. The water lay in thick congealed masses around the conduits and wells, and the buckets were frozen on their stands. The thorough-fares were sheeted with ice, and dangerous to horsemen and vehicles; but the footways were firm and pleasant to the tread.

Here and there, a fire was lighted in the streets, round which ragged urchins and mendicants were collected, roasting fragments of meat stuck upon iron prongs; or quaffing deep draughts of metheglin and ale, out of leathern cups. Crowds were collected in the open places, watching the wonders in the heavens, and drawing auguries from them, chiefly sinister, for most of the beholders thought the signs portended the speedy death of the queen, and the advent of a new monarch from the north a safe and easy interpretation, considering the advanced age and declining health of the illustrious Elizabeth, together with the known appointment of her successor, James of Scotland.

Notwithstanding the early habits of the times, few persons had retired to rest, a universal wish prevailing among the citizens to see the new year in, and welcome the century accompanying it. Lights glimmered in most windows, revealing the holly-sprigs and laurel leaves stuck thickly in their diamond panes; while, whenever a door was opened, a ruddy gleam burst across the street; and a glance inside the dwelling showed its inmates either gathered round the glowing hearth, occupied in mirthful sports – fox-i'-th'-hole, blind-man's-buff, or shoe-the-mare – or seated at the ample board groaning with Christmas cheer.

Music and singing were heard at every comer, and bands of comely damsels, escorted by their sweethearts, went from house to house, bearing huge brown bowls dressed with ribands and rosemary, and filled with a drink called "lamb's-wool", composed of sturdy ale, sweetened with sugar, spiced with nutmeg, and having toasts and burnt crabs floating within it, – a draught from which seldom brought its pretty bearers less than a groat, and occasionally a more valuable coin. Such was the vigil of the year 1600.

On this night, and at the tenth hour, a man of striking and venerable appearance was seen to emerge upon a small wooden balcony, projecting from a bay-window near the top of a picturesque structure situated at the southern extremity of London-bridge.

The old man's beard and hair were as white as snow – the former descending almost to his girdle; so were the thick over- hanging brows that shaded his still piercing eyes. His forehead, was high, bald, and ploughed by innumerable wrinkles. His countenance, despite its death-like paleness, had a noble and majestic cast, and his figure, though worn to the bone by a life of the severest study, and bent by the weight of years, must have been once lofty and commanding. His dress consisted of a doublet and hose of sad-coloured cloth, over which he wore a loose gown of black silk. His head was covered by a square black cap, from beneath which his silver locks strayed over his shoulders.

Known by the name of Doctor Lamb, and addicted to alchemical and philosophical pursuits, this venerable personage was esteemed by the vulgar as little better than a wizard. Strange tales were reported and believed of him. Amongst others, it was said that he possessed a familiar, because he chanced to employ a deformed, crack-brained dwarf, who assisted him in his operations, and whom he appropriately enough denominated Flapdragon.

Doctor Lamb's gaze was fixed intently upon the heavens, and he seemed to be noting the position of the moon with reference to some particular star.

After remaining in this posture for a few minutes, he was about to retire, when a loud crash arrested him, and he turned to see whence it proceeded.

Immediately before him stood the Southwark Gateway – a square stone building, with a round, embattled turret at each corner, and a flat, leaden roof, planted with a forest of poles, fifteen or sixteen feet high, garnished with human heads. To his surprise, the doctor perceived that two of these poles had just been overthrown by a tall man, who was in the act of stripping them of their grisly burdens.

Having accomplished his object, the mysterious plunderer thrust his spoil into a leathern bag with which he was provided, tied its mouth, and was about to take his departure by means of a rope-ladder attached to the battlements, when his retreat was suddenly cut off by the gatekeeper, armed with a halberd, and bearing a lantern, who issued from a door opening upon the leads.

The baffled marauder looked round, and remarking the open window at which Doctor Lamb was stationed, hurled the sack and its contents through it. He then tried to gain the ladder, but was intercepted by the gatekeeper, who dealt him a severe blow on the head with his halberd. The plunderer uttered a loud cry, and attempted to draw his sword; but before he could do so, he received a thrust in the side from his opponent. He then fell, and the gatekeeper would have repeated the blow, if the doctor had not called to him to desist.

"Do not kill him, good Baldred," he cried. "The attempt may not be so criminal as it appears. Doubtless, the mutilated remains which the poor wretch has attempted to carry off, are those of his kindred, and horror at their exposure must have led him to commit the offence."

"It may be, doctor," replied Baldred; "and if so I shall be sorry I have hurt him. But I am responsible for the safe custody of these traitorous relics, and it is as much as my own head is worth to permit their removal."

"I know it," replied Doctor Lamb; "and you are fully justified in what you have done. It may throw some light upon the matter, to know whose miserable remains have been disturbed."

"They were the heads of two rank, papists," replied Baldred, "who were decapitated on Tower Hill, on Saint Nicholas's day, three weeks ago, for conspiring against the queen."

"But their names?" demanded the doctor. "How were they called?"

"They were father and son," replied Baldred; – "Sir Simon Darcy and Master Reginald Darcy. Perchance they were known to your worship?"

"Too well – too well!" replied Doctor Lamb, in a voice of emotion, that startled his hearer. "They were near kinsmen mine own. What is he like who has made this strange attempt?"

"Of a verity, a fair youth," replied Baldred, holding down the lantern. "Heaven grant I have not wounded him to the death! No, his heart still beats. Ha! here are his tablets," he added, taking a small book from his doublet; "these may give the information you seek. You were right in your conjecture, doctor. The name herein inscribed is the same as that borne by the others – Auriol Darcy."

"I see it all," cried Lamb. "It was a pious and praiseworthy deed. Bring the unfortunate youth to my dwelling, Baldred, and you shall be well rewarded. Use despatch, I pray you."

As the gatekeeper essayed to comply, the wounded man groaned deeply, as if in great pain.

"Ring me the weapon with which you smote him," cried Doctor Lamb, in accents of commiseration, "and I will anoint it with the powder of sympathy. His anguish will be speedily abated."

"I know your worship can accomplish wonders," cried Baldred, throwing the halberd into the balcony. "I will do my part as gently as I can."

And as the alchemist took up the weapon, and disappeared through the window, the gatekeeper lifted the wounded man by the shoulders, and conveyed him down a narrow winding staircase to a lower chamber. Though he proceeded carefully, the sufferer was put to excruciating pain; and when Baldred placed him on a wooden bench, and held a lamp towards him, he perceived that his features were darkened and distorted.

"I fear it's all over with him," murmured the gatekeeper; "I shall have a dead body to take to Doctor Lamb. It would be a charity to knock him on the head, rather than let him suffer thus. The doctor passes for a cunning man, but if he can cure this poor youth without seeing him, by the help of his sympathetic ointment, I shall begin to believe, what some folks avouch, that he has relations with the devil."

While Baldred was ruminating in this manner, a sudden and extraordinary change took place in the sufferer. As if by magic, the contraction of the muscles subsided; the features assumed a wholesome hue, and the respiration was no longer laborious. Baldred stared as if a miracle had been wrought.

Now that the countenance of the youth had regained its original expression, the gatekeeper could not help being struck by its extreme beauty. The face was a perfect oval, with regular and delicate features. A short silken moustache covered the upper lip, which was short and proud, and a pointed beard terminated the chin. The hair was black, glossy, and cut short, so as to disclose a highly intellectual expanse of brow.

14

The youth's figure was slight, but admirably proportioned His attire consisted of a black satin doublet, slashed with white, hose of black silk, and a short velvet mantle. His eyes were still closed, and it was difficult to say what effect they might give to the face when they lighted it up; but notwithstanding its beauty, it was impossible not to admit that a strange, sinister, and almost demoniacal expression pervaded the countenance.

All at once, and with as much suddenness as his cure had been effected, the young man started, uttering a piercing cry, and placed his hand to his side.

"Caitiff!" he cried, fixing his blazing eyes on the gatekeeper, "why do you torture me thus? Finish me at once – Oh!"

And overcome by anguish, he sank back again.

"I have not touched you, sir," replied Baldred. "I brought you here to succour you. You will be easier anon. Doctor Lamb must have wiped the halberd," he added to himself.

Another sudden change. The pain fled from the sufferer's countenance, and he became easy as before.

"What have you done to me?" he asked, with a look of gratitude; "the torture of my wound has suddenly ceased, and I feel as if a balm had been dropped into it, Let me remain in this state if you have any pity – or despatch me, for my late agony was almost insupportable."

"You are cared for by one who has greater skill than any surgeon in London," replied Baldred. "If I can manage to transport you to his lodgings, he will speedily heal your wounds."

"Do not delay, then," replied Auriol, faintly; "for though I am free from pain, I feel that my life is ebbing fast away.

"Press this handkerchief to your side, and lean on me." said Baldred. "Doctor Lamb's dwelling is but a step from the gateway – in fact, the first house on the bridge. By the way, the doctor declares he is your kinsman."

"It is the first I ever heard of him," replied Auriol, faintly; "but take me to him quickly, or it will be too late."

In another moment they were at the doctor's door. Baldred tapped against it, and the summons was instantly answered by a diminutive personage, clad in a jerkin of coarse grey serge, and having a leathern apron tied round his waist. This was Flapdragon.

Blear-eyed, smoke-begrimed, lantern-jawed, the poor dwarf seemed as if his whole life had been spent over the furnace. And so, in fact, it had been. He had become little better than a pair of human bellows. In his hand he held the halberd with which Auriol had been wounded.

"So you have been playing the leech., Flapdragon, eh?" cried Baldred. .

"Ay, marry have I," replied the dwarf, with a wild grin, and displaying a wolfish set of teeth, "My master ordered me to smear the halberd with the sympathetic ointment. I obeyed him; rubbed the steel point, first on one side, then on the other; next wiped it; and then smeared it again."

"Whereby you put the patient to exquisite pain," replied Baldred; "but help me to transport him to the laboratory'."

"I know not if the doctor will care to be disturbed," said Flapdragon. "He is busily engaged on a grand operation."

"I will take the risk on myself," said Baldred. "The youth will die if he remains here. See, he has fainted already!"

Thus urged, the dwarf laid down the halberd, and between the two, Auriol was speedily conveyed up a wide oaken staircase to the laboratory. Doctor Lamb was plying the bellows at the furnace, on which a large alembic was placed, and he was so engrossed by his task, that he scarcely noticed the entrance of the others.

"Place the youth on the ground, and rear his head against the chair," he cried, hastily, to the dwarf. "Bathe his brows with the decoction in that crucible. I will attend to him anon. Come to me on the morrow, Baldred, and I will repay thee for thy trouble. I am busy now."

"These relics, doctor," cried the gatekeeper, glancing at the bag, which was lying on the ground, and from which a bald head extruded – "I ought to take them back with me."

"Heed them not – they will be safe in my keeping," cried Doctor Lamb, impatiently; "tomorrow – tomorrow."

Casting a furtive glance round the laboratory, and shrugging his shoulders, Baldred departed; and Flapdragon having bathed the sufferer's temples with the decoction, in obedience to his master's injunctions, turned to inquire what he should do next.

"Be gone!" cried the doctor, so fiercely that the dwarf darted out of the room, clapping the door after him.

Doctor Lamb then applied himself to his task with renewed ardour, and in a few seconds became wholly insensible of the presence of a stranger.

Revived by the stimulant, Auriol presently opened his eyes, and gazing round the room, thought he must be dreaming, so strange and fantastical did all appear. The floor was covered with the implements used by the adept – bolt-heads, crucibles, cucurbites, and retorts, scattered about without any attempt at arrangement. In one corner was a large terrestrial sphere; near it was an astrolabe; and near that a heap of disused glass vessels. On the other side, lay a black, mysterious-looking book, fastened with brazen clasps. Around it, were a ram's horn, a pair of. forceps, a roll of parchment, a pestle and mortar, and a large plate of copper, graven with the mysterious symbols of the Isaical table. Near this was the leathern bag containing the two decapitated

17

heads, one of which had burst forth. On a table, at the further end of the room, stood a large open volume, with parchment leaves, covered with cabbalistical characters, referring to the names of spirits. Near it were two parchment scrolls, written in letters, respectively denominated by the Chaldaic sages, "the Malachim", and "the Passing of the River". One of these scrolls was kept in its place by a skull. An ancient and grotesque-looking brass lamp, with two snake-headed burners, lighted the room. From the ceiling depended a huge scaly sea-monster, with outspread fins, open jaws, garnished with tremendous teeth, and great goggling eyes, Near it hung a celestial sphere. The chimney-piece, which was curiously carved, and projected far into the room, was laden with various implements of Hermetic science. Above it were hung dried bats and flitter-mice, interspersed with the skulls of birds and apes. Attached to the chimney-piece was a horary, sculptured in stone, near which hung a large star-fish. The fireplace was occupied by the furnace, in which, as has been stated, was placed an alembic, communicating by means of a long serpentine pipe with a receiver. Within the room were two skeletons, one of which, placed behind a curtain in the deep embrasure of the window, where its polished bones glistened in the white moonlight, had a horrible effect. The other enjoyed more comfortable quarters near the chimney, its fleshless feet dangling down in the smoke arising from the furnace.

Doctor Lamb, meanwhile, steadily pursued his task, though he ever and anon paused, to fling certain roots and drugs upon the charcoal. As he did this, various-coloured flames broke forth – now blue, now green, now blood-red.

Tinged by these fires, the different objects in the chamber seemed to take other forms, and to become instinct with animation. The gourd-shaped cucurbites were transformed into great bloated toads bursting with venom; the long-necked bolt-heads became monstrous serpents; the worm-like pipes turned into adders; the alembics looked like plumed helmets; the characters on the Isaical table, and those on the parchments, seemed traced in fire, and to be ever changing; the sea-monster bellowed and roared, and, flapping his fins, tried to burst from his hook; the skeletons wagged their jaws, and raised their fleshless fingers in mockery, while blue lights burnt in their eyeless sockets; the bellows became a prodigious bat fanning the fire with its wings: and the old Alchemist assumed the appearance of the arch-fiend presiding over a witches' sabbath.

Auriol's brain reeled, and he pressed his hand to his eyes, to exclude these phantasms from his sight. But even thus they pursued him; and he imagined he could hear the infernal riot going on around him.

Suddenly, he was roused by a loud joyful cry, and, uncovering his eyes, he beheld Doctor Lamb pouring the contents of the matrass – a bright, transparent liquid – into a small phial. Having carefully secured the bottle with a glass stopper, the old man held it towards the light, and gazed at it with rapture. "At length," he exclaimed aloud – "at length, the great work is achieved. With the birth of the century now expiring I first saw light, and the draught I hold in my hand shall enable me to see the opening of centuries and centuries to come. Composed of the lunar stones, the solar stones, and the mercurial stones – prepared according to the instructions of the Rabbi Ben Lucca, namely, by the separation of the pure from the impure, the volatilisation of the fixed, and the fixing of the volatile; this elixir shall renew my youth, like that of the eagle, and give me length of days greater than any patriarch ever enjoyed."

While thus speaking, he held up the sparkling liquid, and gazed at it like a Persian worshipping the sun.

"To live for ever!" he cried, after a pause – "to escape the jaws of death just when they are opening to devour me! – to be free from all accidents! – 'tis a glorious thought! Ha! I bethink me, the rabbi said there was *one* peril against which the elixir could not guard me – *one* vulnerable point; by which, like the heel of Achilles, death might reach me! What is it? – where can it lie?"

And he relapsed into deep thought.

"This uncertainty will poison all my happiness," he continued; "I shall live in constant dread, as of an invisible enemy. But no matter! Perpetual life! – perpetual youth! – what more need be desired?"

"What more, indeed!" cried Auriol.

"Ha!" exclaimed the doctor, suddenly recollecting the wounded man, and concealing the phial beneath his gown.

"Your caution is vain, doctor," said Auriol. "I have heard what you have uttered. You fancy. you have discovered the elixir vitae."

"Fancy, I have discovered it!" cried Doctor Lamb. "The matter is past all doubt. I am the possessor of the wondrous secret, which the greatest philosophers of all ages have sought to discover – the miraculous preservative of the body against decay."

"The man who brought me hither told me you were my kinsman," said Auriol. "Is it so?"

"It is," replied the doctor, "and you shall now learn the connection that subsists between us. Look at that ghastly relic," he added, pointing to the head protruding from the bag, "that was once my son Simon. His son's head is within the sack – your father's head – so that four generations are brought together,"

"Gracious Heaven!" exclaimed the young man, raising himself on his elbow. "You, then, are my great-grandsire. My father supposed you had died in his infancy. An old tale runs in the family that you were charged with sorcery, and fled to avoid the stake."

"It is true that I fled, and took the name I bear at present," replied the old man, "but I need scarcely say that the charge brought against me was false. I have devoted myself to abstrusest science; have held commune with the stars; and have wrested the most hidden secrets from Nature – but that is all. Two crimes alone have stained my soul, but both, I trust, have been expiated by repentance."

"Were they deeds of blood?" asked Auriol.

"One was so," replied Darcy, with a shudder. "It was a cowardly and treacherous deed, aggravated by the basest ingratitude. Listen, and you shall hear how it chanced. A Roman rabbi, named Ben Lucca, skilled in Hermetic science, came to this city. His fame reached me, and I sought him out, offering myself as his disciple. For months, I

20

remained with him in his laboratory working at the furnace, and poring over mystic lore. One night, he showed me that volume, and, pointing to a page within it, said: 'Those characters contain the secret of confecting the elixir of life. I now explain them to you; and afterwards we will proceed to the operation.' With this, he unfolded the mystery; but he bade me observe, that the menstruum was defective on one point. Wherefore, he said, 'there will still be peril from some hidden cause.' Oh, with what greediness I drank in his words! How I gazed at the mystic characters, as he explained their import! What visions floated before me of perpetual youth and enjoyment. At that moment a demon whispered in my ear, – "This secret must be thine own. No one else must possess it'."

"Ha!" exclaimed Auriol, starting.

"The evil thought was no sooner conceived than acted upon," pursued Darcy. "Instantly drawing my poniard, I plunged it to the rabbi's heart. But mark what followed. His blood fell upon the book, and obliterated the characters; nor could I by any effort of memory recall the composition of the elixir."

"When did you regain the secret?" asked Auriol, curiously.

"Tonight," replied Darcy – "within this hour. For nigh fifty years after that fatal night I have been making fruitless experiments. A film of blood has obscured my mental sight. I have proceeded by calcitration, solution, putrefaction – have produced the oils which will fix crude mercury, and convert all bodies into sol and luna; but I have ever failed in fermenting the stone into the true elixir. Tonight, it came into my head to wash the blood-stained page containing the secret with a subtle liquid. I did so; and doubting the efficacy of the experiment, left it to work, while I went forth to breath the air at my window. My eyes were cast upwards, and I was struck with the malignant aspect of my star. How to reconcile this with the good fortune which has just befallen me, I know not – but so it was. At this juncture, your rash, but pious attempt occurred. Having discovered our relationship, and enjoined the gatekeeper to bring you hither, I returned to my old laboratory. On glancing towards the mystic volume, what was my surprise to see the page free from blood!"

21

Auriol uttered a slight exclamation, and gazed at the book with superstitious awe.

"The sight was so surprising, that I dropped the sack I had brought with me," pursued Darcy. "Fearful of again losing the secret, I nerved myself to the task, and placing fuel on the fire, dismissed my attendant with brief injunctions relative to you. I then set to work. How I have succeeded, you perceive. I hold in my hand the treasure I have so long sought – so eagerly coveted. The whole world's wealth should not purchase it from me."

Auriol gazed earnestly at his aged relative, but he said nothing.

"In a few moments I shall be as full of vigour and activity as yourself," continued Darcy. "We shall be no longer the great-grandsire and his descendant, but friends – companions – equals, – equals in age, strength, activity, beauty, fortune – for youth is fortune ha! ha! Methinks I am already young again!"

"You spoke of two crimes with which your conscience was burdened," remarked Auriol. "You have mentioned but one."

"The other was not so foul as that I have described," replied Darcy, in an altered tone, "in as much as it was unintentional, and occasioned by no base motive. My wife, your ancestress, was a most lovely woman, and so passionately was I enamoured of her, that I tried by every art to heighten and preserve her beauty. I fed her upon the flesh of capons, nourished with vipers; caused her to steep her lovely limbs in baths distilled from roses and violets; and had recourse to the most potent cosmetics. At last I prepared a draught from poisons – yes, *poisons* – the effect of which I imagined would be wondrous. She drank it, and expired horribly disfigured. Conceive my despair at beholding the fair image of my idolatry destroyed – defaced by my hand. In my frenzy I should have laid violent hands upon myself, if I had not been restrained. Love may again rule my heart – beauty may again dazzle my eyes, but I shall never more feel the passion I entertained for my lost Amice – never more behold charms equal to hers."

And he pressed his hand to his face.

"The mistake you then committed should serve as a warning," replied Auriol. "What if it be poison you have now confected? Try a few drops of it on some animal."

"No – no; it is the true elixir," replied Darcy. "Not a drop must be wasted. You will witness its effect anon. Like the snake, I shall cast my slough, and come forth younger than I was at twenty."

"Meantime, I beseech you to render me some assistance," groaned Auriol, "or, while you are preparing for immortality, I shall expire before your eyes."

"Be not afraid," replied Darcy; "you shall take no harm. I will care for you presently; and I understand leechcraft so well, that I will answer for your speedy and perfect recovery."

"Drink, then, to it!" cried Auriol.

"I know not what stays my hand," said the old man, raising the phial; "but now that immortality is in my reach, I dare not grasp it."

"Give me the potion, then," cried Auriol.

"Not for worlds," rejoined Darcy, hugging the phial to his breast. "No; I will be young again – rich – happy. I will go forth into the world – I will bask in the smiles of beauty – I will feast, revel, sing – life shall be one perpetual round of enjoyment. Now for the trial – ha!" and, as he raised the potion towards his lips, a sudden pang shot across his heart. "What is this?" he cried, staggering. "Can death assail me when I am just about to enter upon perpetual life? Help me, good grandson! Place the phial to my lips. Pour its contents down my throat – quick! quick!"

"I am too weak to stir," groaned Auriol. "You have delayed it too long."

"Oh, Heavens! we shall both perish," shrieked Darcy, vainly endeavouring to raise his palsied arm, – "perish with the blissful shore in view."

And he sank backwards, and would have fallen to the ground if he had not caught at the terrestrial sphere for support.

"Help me – help me!" he screamed, fixing a glance of unutterable anguish on his relative.

"It is worth the struggle," cried Auriol. And, by a great effort, he raised himself, and staggered towards the old man.

"Saved – saved!" shrieked Darcy. "Pour it down my throat. An instant, and all will be well."

"Think you I have done this for you?" cried Auriol, snatching the potion; "no – no."

And, supporting himself against the furnace, he placed the phial to his lips, and eagerly drained its contents.

The old man seemed paralysed by the action, but kept his eye fixed upon the youth till he had drained the elixir to the last drop. He then uttered a piercing cry, threw up his arm, and fell heavily back-wards.

Dead – dead!

Flashes of light passed before Auriol's eyes, and strange noises smote his ears. For a moment he was bewildered as with wine, and laughed and sang discordantly like a madman. Every object reeled and danced around him. The glass vessels and jars clashed their brittle sides together, yet remained uninjured; the furnace breathed forth flames and mephitic vapours; the spiral worm of the alembic became red hot, and seemed filled with molten lead; the pipe of the bolt-head ran blood; the sphere of the earth rolled along the floor, and rebounded from the wail as if impelled by a giant hand; the skeletons grinned and gibbered; so did the death's-head on the table; so did the skulls against the chimney; the monstrous sea-fish belched forth fire and smoke; the bald decapitated head opened its eyes, and fixed them, with a stony glare, on the young man; while the dead alchemist shook his hand menacingly at him.

Unable to bear these accumulated horrors, Auriol became, for a short space, insensible. On recovering, all was still. The lights within the lamp had expired; but the bright moonlight, streaming through the window, fell upon the rigid features of the unfortunate alchemist, and on the cabalistic characters of the open volume beside him. Eager to test the effect of the elixir, Auriol put his hand to his side. All traces of the wound were gone; nor did he experience the slightest pain in any other part of his body. On the contrary, he seemed endowed with pre-ternatural strength. His breast dilated with rapture, and he longed to expand his joy in active notion. Striding over the body of his aged relative, he threw open the window. As he did so joyous peals burst from surrounding churches, announcing the arrival of the new year. While listening to this clamour, Auriol gazed at the populous and pic-turesque city stretched out before him, and bathed in the moonlight.

"A hundred years hence," he thought, "and scarcely one soul of the thousands within those houses will be living, save myself. A hun-dred years after that, and their children's children will be gone to the grave. But I shall live on – shall live through all changes – all customs – all time. What revelations I shall then have to make, if I should dare to disclose them!"

As he ruminated thus, the skeleton hanging near him was swayed by the wind, and its bony fingers came in contact with his cheek. A dread idea was suggested by the occurrence.

"There is one peril to be avoided," he thought; "ONE PERIL! – what is it? Pshaw! I will think no more of it. It may never arise. I will be gone. This place fevers me."

With this, he left the laboratory, and hastily descending the stairs, at the foot of which he found Flapdragon, passed out of the house.

Book the First – Ebba

I. The Ruined House in the Vauxhall Road

One night, in the spring of 1830, two men issued from a low, obscurely situated public-house, near Millbank, and shaped their course apparently in the direction of Vauxhall-bridge. Avoiding the footpath near the river, they moved stealthily along the further side of the road, where the open ground offered them an easy means of flight, in case such a course should he found expedient. So far as it could be discerned by the glimpses of the moon, which occasionally shone forth from a rack of heavy clouds, the appearance of these personages was not much in their favour. Haggard features, stamped deeply with the characters of crime and debauchery; fierce, restless eyes; beards of several days' growth; wild, unkempt heads of hair, formed their chief personal characteristics; while sordid and ragged clothes; shoes without soles; and old hats without crowns, constituted the sum of their apparel.

One of them was tall and gaunt, with large hands and feet; but despite his meagreness, he evidently possessed great strength: the other was considerably shorter, but broad-shouldered, bow-legged, long-armed, and altogether a most formidable ruffian. This fellow had high cheekbones, a long aquiline nose, and a coarse mouth and chin, in which the animal greatly predominated. He had a stubby red beard, with sandy hair, white brows and eyelashes. The countenance of the other was dark and repulsive, and covered with blotches, the result of habitual intemperance. His eyes had a leering and malignant look. A handkerchief spotted with blood, and tied across his brow, contrasted strongly with his matted black hair, and increased his natural appearance of ferocity. The shorter ruffian carried a mallet upon his shoulder, and his companion concealed something beneath the breast of his coat, which afterwards proved to be a dark lantern.

Not a word passed between them; but keeping a vigilant lookout, they trudged on with quick, shambling steps. A few sounds arose from the banks of the river, and there was now and then a plash in the water, or a distant cry, betokening some passing craft; but generally all was profoundly still. The quaint, Dutch-looking structures on the opposite bank, the line of coal-barges and lighters moored to the strand, the great timber-yards and coal-yards, the brewhouses, gasworks, and waterworks, could only be imperfectly discerned; but the moonlight fell clear upon the ancient towers of Lambeth Palace, and on the neighbouring church. The same glimmer also ran like a silver belt across the stream, and revealed the great, stern, fortress-like pile of the Penitentiary – perhaps the most dismal-looking structure in the whole metropolis. The world of habitations beyond this melancholy prison were buried in darkness. The two men, however, thought nothing of these things, and saw nothing of them; but, on arriving within a couple of hundred yards of the bridge, suddenly, as if by previous concert, quitted the road, and, leaping a rail, ran across a field, and plunged into a hollow formed by a dried pit, where they came to a momentary halt.

"You ain't a-been a-gammonin' me in this matter, Tinker?" observed the shorter individual. "The cove's sure to come?"

"Why, you can't expect me to answer for another as I can for myself, Sandman," replied the other; "but if his own word's to be taken for it, he's sartin to be there. I heerd him say, as plainly as I'm a-speakin' to you, – 'I'll be here tomorrow night at the same hour -'"

"And that wos one o'clock?" said the Sandman.

"Thereabouts," replied the other.

"And who did he say that to?" demanded the Sandman.

"To hisself, I s'pose," answered the Tinker; "for, as I told you afore, I could see no one vith him."

"Do you think he's one of our perfession?" inquired the Sandman.

"Bless you! no – that he hain't," returned the Tinker. "He's a reg'lar slap-up swell."

"That's no reason at all," said the Sandman. "Many a first-rate svell practises in our line. But he can't be in his right mind to come to such a ken as that, and go on as you mentions."

"As to that I can't say," replied the Tinker; "and it don't much matter, as far as ve're consarned."

"Devil a bit," rejoined the Sandman, "except – you're sure it worn't a sperrit, Tinker. I've heerd say that this crib is haanted, and though I don't fear no livin' man, a ghost's a different sort of customer."

"Vell, you'll find our svell raal flesh and blood, you may depend upon it," replied the Tinker. "So come along, and don't let's be frightenin' ourselves vith ould vimen's tales."

With this they emerged from the pit, crossed the lower part of the field, and entered a narrow thoroughfare, skirted by a few detached houses, which brought them into the Vauxhall-bridge road.

Here they kept on the side of the street most in shadow, and crossed over whenever they came to a lamp. By-and-by, two watchmen were seen advancing from Belvoir-terrace, and, as the guardians of the night drew near, the ruffians crept into an alley to let them pass. As soon as the coast was clear, they ventured forth, and quickening their pace, came to a row of deserted and dilapidated houses. This was their destination.

The range of habitations in question, more than a dozen in number, were, in all probability, what is vulgarly called "in Chancery", and shared the fate of most property similarly circumstanced. They were in a sad ruinous state – unroofed, without windows and floors. The bare walls were alone left standing, and these were in a very tumbledown condition. These neglected dwellings served as receptacles for old iron, blocks of stone and wood, and other ponderous matters. The aspect of the whole place was so dismal and suspicious, that it was generally avoided by passengers after nightfall.

Skulking along the blank and dreary walls, the Tinker, who was now a little in advance, stopped before a door, and pushing it open, entered the dwelling. His companion followed him.

The extraordinary and incongruous assemblage of objects which met the gaze of the Sandman, coupled with the deserted appearance of the place, produced an effect upon his hardy but superstitious nature.

Looking round, he beheld huge mill-stones, enormous water-wheels, boilers of steam-engines, iron vats, cylinders, cranes, iron pumps of the strangest fashion, a gigantic pair of wooden scales, old iron safes, old boilers, old gas-pipes, old water-pipes, cracked old bells, old birdcages, old plates of iron, old pulleys, ropes, and rusty chains, huddled and heaped together in the most fantastic disorder. In the midst of the chaotic mass frowned the bearded and colossal head of Neptune, which had once decorated the forepart of a man-of-war. Above it, on a sort of framework, lay the prostrate statue of a nymph, together with a bust of Fox, the nose of the latter being partly demolished, and the eyes knocked in. Above these, three garden divinities laid their heads amicably together. On the left stood a tall Grecian warrior, minus the head and right hand. The whole was surmounted by an immense ventilator, stuck on the end of an iron rod, ascending, like a lightning-conductor, from the steam-engine pump.

Seen by the transient light of the moon, the various objects above enumerated produced a strange effect upon the beholder's imagination. There was a mixture of the grotesque and terrible about them. Nor was the building itself devoid of a certain influence upon his mind. The ragged brickwork, over-grown with weeds, took with him the semblance of a human face, and seemed to keep a wary eye on what was going forward below.

A means of crossing from one side of the building to the other, without descending into the vault beneath, was afforded by a couple of planks; though as the wall on the farther side was some feet higher than that near at hand, and the planks were considerably bent, the passage appeared hazardous.

Glancing round for a moment, the Tinker leaped into the cellar, and, unmasking his lantern, showed a sort of hiding-place, between a bulk of timber and a boiler, to which he invited his companion.

The Sandman jumped down.

"The ale I drank at the 'Two Fighting Cocks' has made me feel drowsy, Tinker," he remarked, stretching himself on the bulk; "I'll just take a snooze. Vake me up if I snore – or ven our sperrit appears."

The Tinker replied in the affirmative; and the other had just become lost to consciousness, when he received a nudge in the side, and his companion whispered – "He's here!"

"Vhere – vhere?" demanded the Sandman, in some trepidation.

"Look up, and you'll see him," replied the other.

Slightly altering his position, the Sandman caught sight of a figure standing upon the planks above them. It was that of a young man. His hat was off, and his features, exposed to the full radiance of the moon, looked deathly pale, and though handsome, had a strange sinister expression. He was tall, slight, and well-proportioned; and the general cut of his attire, the tightly buttoned, single-breasted coat, together with the moustache upon his lip, gave him a military air.

"He seems a-valkin' in his sleep," muttered the Sandman. "He's a-speakin' to some von unwisible."

"Hush hush!" whispered the other. "let's hear wot he's a-sayin'."

"Why have you brought me here?" cried the young man, in a voice so hollow that it thrilled his auditors. "What is to be done?"

"It makes my blood run cold to hear him," whispered the Sandman. "Vot d'ye think he sees?"

"Why do you not speak to me?" cried the young man -"why do you beckon me forward? Well, I obey. I will follow you." And he moved slowly across the plank.

"See, he's a-goin' through that door," cried the Tinker. "let's foller him."

"I don't half like it," replied the Sandman, his teeth chattering with apprehension. "We shall see summat as'll take avay our senses."

"Tut!" cried the Tinker; "it's only a sleepy-valker. Wot are you afeerd on?"

With this he vaulted upon the planks, and peeping cautiously out of the open door to which they led, saw the object of his scrutiny enter the adjoining house through a broken window.

Making a sign to the Sandman, who was close at his heels, the Tinker crept forward on all fours, and, on reaching the window, raised himself just sufficiently to command the interior of the dwelling. Unfortunately for him, the moon was at this moment obscured, and he could distinguish nothing except the dusky outline of the various objects with which the place was filled, and which were nearly of the same kind as those of the neighbouring habitation. He listened intently, but not the slightest sound reached his ears.

After some time spent in this way, he began to fear the young man must have departed, when all at once a piercing scream resounded through the dwelling. Some heavy matter was dislodged, with a thundering crash, and footsteps were heard approaching the window,

Hastily retreating to their former hiding-place, the Tinker and his companion had scarcely regained it, when the young man again appeared on the plank. His demeanour had undergone a fearful change. He staggered rather than walked, and his countenance was even paler than before. Having crossed the plank, he took his way along the top of the broken wall towards the door.

"Now, then, Sandman!" cried the Tinker; "now's your time!"

The other nodded, and, grasping his mallet with a deadly and determined purpose, sprang noiselessly upon the wall, and overtook his intended victim just before he gained the door.

Hearing a sound behind him, the young man turned, and only just became conscious of the presence of the Sandman, when the mallet descended upon his head, and he fell crushed and senseless to the ground.

"The work's done!" cried the Sandman to his companion, who instantly came up with the dark lantern; "let's take him below, and strip him."

"Agreed," replied the Tinker; "but first let's see wot he has got in his pockets."

"Vith all my 'art," replied the Sandman, searching the clothes of the victim. "A reader! – I hope it's well lined. We'll examine it below. The body 'ud tell awkvard tales if any von should chance to peep in."

"Shall we strip him here?" said the Tinker. "Now the darkey shines on 'em, you see what famous togs the cull has on."

"Do you vant to have us scragged, fool?" cried the Sandman, springing into the vault "Hoist him down here."

With this, he placed the wounded man's legs over his own shoulders, and, aided by his comrade, was in the act of heaving down the body, when the street-door suddenly flew open, and a stout individual, attended by a couple of watchmen, appeared at it.

'There the villains are!" shouted the newcomer. They have been murderin' a gentleman. Seize 'em – seize 'em!"

And, as he spoke, he discharged a pistol, the ball from which whistled past the ears of the Tinker.

Without waiting for another salute of the same kind, which might possibly be nearer its mark, the ruffian kicked the lantern into the vault, and sprang after the Sandman, who had already. disappeared.

Acquainted with the intricacies of the place, the Tinker guided his companion through a hole into an adjoining vault, whence they scaled a wail, got into the next house, and passing through an open window, made good their retreat, while the watchmen were vainly searching for them under every bulk and piece of iron.

"Here, watchmen!" cried the stout individual, who had acted as leader; "never mind the villains just now, but help me to convey this poor young gentleman to my house, where proper assistance can be rendered him. He still breathes; but he has received a terrible blow on the head. I hope his skull ain't broken."

"It is to be hoped it ain't, Mr. Thorneycroft," replied the foremost watchman; "but them was two desperate char*ac*ters, as ever I see, and capable of any ahtterosity."

"What a frightful scream I heard to be sure!" cried Mr. Thorney-croft. "I was certain sornethin' dreadful was goin' on. It was fortunate I wasn't gone to bed; and still more fortunate you happened to be comin' up at the time. But we mustn't stand chatterin' here. Bring the poor young gentleman along."

Preceded by Mr. Thorneycroft, the watchmen carried the wounded man across the road towards a small house, the door of which was held open by a female servant, with a candle in her band. The poor woman uttered a cry of horror as the body was brought in.

"Don't be cryin' out in that way, Peggy," cried Mr. Thorneycroft, "but go and get me some brandy. Here, watchmen, lay the poor young gentleman down on the sofa – there, gently, gently. And now, one of you run to Wheeler-street, and fetch Mr. Howell, the surgeon. Less noise, Peggy – less noise, or you'll waken Miss Ebba, and I wouldn't have her disturbed for the world."

With this, he snatched the bottle of brandy from the maid filled a wine-glass with the spirit, and poured it down the throat of the wounded man. A stifling sound followed, and after struggling violently for respiration for a few seconds, the patient opened his eyes.

II. The Dog-Fancier

The Rookery! Who that has passed Saint Giles's, on the way to the city, or corning from it, but has caught a glimpse, through some narrow opening, of its squalid habitations, and wretched and ruffianly occupants! Who but must have been struck with amazement, that such a huge receptacle of vice and crime should be allowed to exist in the very heart of the metropolis, like an ulcerated spot, capable of tainting the whole system! Of late, the progress of improvement has caused its removal; but whether any less cogent motive would have abated the nuisance, may be questioned. For years the evil was felt, and complained of, but no effort was made to remedy it, or to cleanse these worse than Augean stables. As the place is now partially, if not altogether, swept away, and a wide and airy street passes through the midst of its foul recesses, a slight sketch may be given of its former appearance.

Entering a narrow street, guarded by posts and crossbars, a few steps from the crowded thoroughfare brought you into a frightful region, the refuge, it was easy to perceive, of half the lawless characters infesting the metropolis. The coarsest ribaldry assailed your ears, and noisome odours afflicted your sense of smell. As you advanced, picking your way through kennels flowing with filth, or over putrescent heaps of rubbish and oyster-shells, all the repulsive and hideous features of the place were displayed before you. There was something savagely picturesque in the aspect of the place, but its features were too loathsome to be regarded with any other feeling than disgust. The houses looked as sordid, and as thickly crusted with the leprosy of vice, as their tenants. Horrible habitations they were, in truth. Many of them were without windows, and where the frames were left, brown paper or tin supplied the place of glass; some even wanted doors, and no effort was made to conceal the squalor within. On the contrary, it seemed to be intruded on observation. Miserable rooms, almost destitute of furniture; floors and walls caked with dirt, or decked with coarse flaring prints; shameless and abandoned-looking women; children without shoes and stockings, and with scarcely a rag to their backs: these were the chief objects that met the view. Of men, few were visible – the majority being out on business, it is to be presumed; but where a solitary straggler was seen, his sinister looks and mean attire were in perfect keeping with the spot. So thickly inhabited were these wretched dwellings, that every chamber, from garret to cellar, swarmed with inmates. As to the cellars, they looked like dismal caverns, which a wild beast would shun. Clothes-lines were hung from house to house, festooned with every kind of garment. Out of the main street branched several alleys and passages, all displaying the same degree of misery, or, if possible, worse, and teeming with occupants. Personal security, however, forbade any attempt to track these labyrinths; but imagination, after the specimen afforded, could easily picture them. It was impossible to move a step without insult or annoyance. Every human being seemed brutalised and degraded; and the women appeared utterly lost to decency, and made the street ring with their cries, their quarrels, and their imprecations. It was a positive relief to escape from this hotbed of crime to the world without, and breathe a purer atmosphere.

Such being the aspect of the Rookery in the daytime, what must it have been when crowded with its denizens at night! Yet at such an hour it will now be necessary to enter its penetralia.

After escaping from the ruined house in the Vauxhall-road, the two ruffians shaped their course towards Saint Giles's, running the greater part of the way, and reaching the Broadway Just as the church clock struck two. Darting into a narrow alley, and heedless of any obstructions they encountered in their path, they entered a somewhat wider cross-street, which they pursued for a short distance, and then struck into an entry, at the bottom of which was a swing door that admitted them into a small court, where they found a dwarfish person wrapped in a tattered watchman's great-coat, seated on a stool with a horn lantern in his hand and a cutty in his mouth, the glow of which lighted up his hard, withered features. This was the deputy-porter of the lodging-house they were about to enter. Addressing him by the name of Old Parr, the ruffians passed on, and lifting the latch of another door, entered a sort of kitchen, at the farther end of which blazed a cheerful fire, with a large copper kettle boiling upon it. On one side of the room was a deal table, round which several men of sinister aspect and sordid attire were collected, playing at cards. A smaller table of the same material stood near the fire, and opposite it was a staircase leading to the upper rooms. The place was dingy and dirty in the extreme, the floors could not have been scoured for years, and the walls were begrimed with filth. In one corner, with his head resting on a heap of coals and coke, lay a boy almost as black as a chimney-sweep, fast asleep. He was the waiter. The principal light was afforded by a candle stuck against the wall, with a tin reflector behind it. Before the fire, with his back turned towards it, stood a noticeable individual, clad in a velveteen jacket, with ivory buttons, a striped waistcoat, drab knees, a faded black silk neckcloth tied in a great bow, and a pair of ancient Wellingtons ascending half-way up his legs, which looked disproportionately thin when compared with the upper part of his square, robustious, and somewhat pursy frame. His face was broad, jolly, and good-humoured, with a bottle-shaped nose, fleshy lips, and light grey eyes, glistening with cunning and roguery. His hair, which dangled in long flakes over his ears and neck, was of a dunnish red, as were also his whiskers and beard. A superannuated white castor, with a black hatband round it, was cocked knowingly on one side of his head, and gave him a flashy and sporting look. His particular vocation was made manifest by the number of dogs he had about him. A beautiful black-tan spaniel, of Charles the Second's breed, popped its short snubby nose and long silken ears out of each coat-pocket. A pug was thrust into his breast, and he carried an exquisite Blenheim under either arm. At his feet reposed an Isle of Skye terrier, and a partly cropped French poodle, of snowy whiteness, with a red worsted riband round his throat. This person, it need scarcely be said, was a dog-fancier, or, in other words, a dealer in, and a stealer of dogs, as well as a practiser of all the tricks connected with that nefarious trade. His self-satisfied air made it evident he thought himself a smart clever fellow, – and adroit and knavish he was, no doubt, – while his droll, plausible, and rather winning manners, helped him materially to impose upon his customers. His real name was Taylor, but he was known among his companions by the appellation of Ginger. On the entrance of the Sandman and the Tinker, he nodded familiarly to them, and with a sly look inquired – "Vell, my 'arties – wot luck?"

"Oh, pretty middling'," replied the Sandman, gruffly.

And seating himself at the table, near the fire, he kicked up the lad, who was lying fast asleep on the coals, and bade him fetch a pot of half-and-half. The Tinker took a place beside him, and they waited in silence the arrival of the liquor, which, when it came, was disposed of at a couple of pulls; while Mr. Ginger, seeing they were engaged, sauntered towards the card-table, attended by his four-footed companions.

"And now," said the Sandman, unable to control his curiosity longer, and taking out his pocket-book, "we'll see what fortun' has given us."

So saying, he unclasped the pocket-book, while the Tinker bent over him in eager curiosity. But their search for money was fruitless. Not a single bank-note was forthcoming. There were several memoranda and slips of paper, a few cards, and an almanack for the year – that was, all. It was a great disappointment.

"So we've had all this trouble for nuffin', and nearly got shot into the bargain," cried the Sandman, slapping down the book on the table with an oath. "I vish I'd never undertaken the job."

"Don't let's give it up in sich an 'urry," replied the Tinker; "summat may be made on it yet. Let's look over them papers."

"Look 'em over yourself," rejoined the Sandman, pushing the book towards him. "I've done wi' 'em. Here, lazy-bones, bring two glasses' o' rum-and-water – stiff, d'ye hear?"

While the sleepy youth bestirred himself to obey these injunctions, the Tinker read over every memorandum in the pocket-book, and then proceeded carefully to examine the different scraps of paper with which it was filled. Not content with one perusal, he looked them all over again, and then began to rub his hands with great glee.

"Wot's the matter?" cried the Sandman, who had lighted a cutty, and was quietly smoking it. "Wot's the row, eh?"

"Vy, this is it," replied the Tinker, unable to contain his satisfaction; "there's secrets contained in this here pocket-book as'll be worth a hundred pound and better to us. We ha'n't had our trouble for nuffin'."

"Glad to hear it!" said the Sandman, looking hard at him. "Wot kind o' secrets are they?"

"Vy, *hangin' secrets*," replied the Tinker, with mysterious emphasis. "He seems to be a terrible chap, and to have committed murder wholesale."

"Wholesale!" echoed the Sandman, removing the pipe from his lips. "That sounds awful. But what a precious donkey he must be to register his crimes i' that way."

"He didn't expect the pocket-book to fall into our hands," said the Tinker.

"Werry likely not," replied the Sandman; "but somebody else might see it. I repeat, he must be a fool. S'pose we wos to make a entry of everythin' we does. Wot a nice balance there'd be agin us ven our accounts comed to be wound up."

"Ourn is a different bus'ness altogether," replied the Tinker. "This seems a werry mysterious sort o' person. Wot age should you take him to be?"

"Vy, five-an' twenty at the outside," replied the Sandman.

"Five-an'-sixty 'ud be nearer the mark," replied the Tinker. "There's dates as far back as that."

"Five-an'-sixty devils!" cried the Sandman; "there must be some mistake i' the reckonin' there."

"No, it's all clear an' reg'lar," rejoined the other; "and that doesn't seem to be the end of it neither. I looked over the papers twice, and one, dated 1780, refers to some other dokiments."

"They must relate to his granddad, then," said the Sandman; "it's impossible they can refer to him."

"But I tell 'ee they do refer to him" said the Tinker, somewhat angrily, at having his assertion denied; "at least, if his own word's to be taken. Anyhow, these papers is waluable to us. If no one else believes in 'em, it's clear he believes in 'em hisself, and will be glad to buy 'em from us."

"That's a view o' the case worthy of an Old Bailey lawyer," replied the Sandman. "Wot's the gemman's name?"

"The name on the card is Auriol Darcy," replied the Tinker.

"Any address?" asked the Sandman.

The Tinker shook his head.

"That's unlucky agin," said the Sandman. "Ain't there no sort o' clue?"

"None votiver, as I can perceive," said the Tinker.

"Vy, zounds, then, ve're jist vere ve started from," cried the Sandman. "But it don't matter. There's not much chance o' makin' a bargin vith him. The crak o' the skull I gave him has done his bus'ness."

"Nuffin' o' the kind," replied the Tinker. "He alvays recovers from every kind of accident."

"Alvays recovers!" exclaimed the Sandman, in amazement. "Wot a constitootion he must have."

"Surprisin'!" replied the Tinker; "he never suffers from injuries – at least, not much; never grows old; and never expects to die; for he mentions wot he intends doin' a hundred years hence."

"Oh, he's a lu-nattic!" exclaimed the Sandman, "a downright lu-nattic; and that accounts for his wisitin' that 'ere ruined house, and a-fancyin' he heerd some one talk to him. He's mad, depend upon it. That is, if I ain't cured him."

"'I'm of a different opinion," said the Tinker.

"And so am I," said Mr. Ginger, who had approached unobserved, and overheard the greater part of their discourse.

"Vy, vot can you know about it, Ginger?" said the Sandman, looking up, evidently rather annoyed.

"I only know this," replied Ginger, "that you've got a good case, and if you'll let me into it, I'll engage to make summat of it."

"Vell, I'm agreeable," said the Sandman.

"And so am I," added the Tinker.

"Not that I pays much regard to wot you've bin a readin' in his papers," pursued Ginger; "the gemman's evidently half-cracked, if he ain't cracked altogether – but he's jist the person to work upon. He fancies hisself immortal – eh?"

"Exactly so," replied the Tinker.

"And he also fancies he's 'committed a lot o' murders?" pursued Ginger.

"A desperate lot," replied the Tinker.

"Then he'll be glad to buy those papers at any price," said Ginger. "Ve'll deal vith him in regard to the pocketbook, as I deals vith regard to a dog – ask a price for its restitootion.".

"We must find him out first," said the Sandman.

"There's no difficulty in that," rejoined Ginger. "You must be constantly on the look-out. You're sure to meet him some time or other'."

"That's true," replied the Sandman; "and there's no fear of his knowin' us, for the werry moment he looked round I knocked him on the head."

"Arter all," said the Tinker, "there's no branch o' the perfession so safe as yours, Ginger. The law is favourable to you, and the beaks is afeerd to touch you. I think I shall turn dog-fancier myself."

"It's a good business," replied Ginger, "but it requires a hedica-tion. As I wos sayin', we gets a high price sometimes for restorin' a favourite, especially ven ve've a soft-hearted lady to deal vith. There's some vimen as fond o' dogs as o' their own childer, and ven ve gets one o' their precious pets, ve makes 'em ransom it as the brigands you see at the Adelphi or the Surrey sarves their prisoners, threatenin' to send first an ear, and then a paw, or a tail, and so on. I'll tell you wot happened t'other day. There wos a lady – a Miss Vite – as was desper-ate fond of her dog. It wos a ugly warmint, but no matter for that – the creater had gained her heart. Vell, she lost it; and, somehow or other, I found it. She vos in great trouble, and a friend o' mine calls to say she can have the dog agin, but she must pay eight pound for it. She thinks this dear, and a friend o' her own adwises her to wait, sayin' better terms will be offered; so I sends vord by my friend that if she don't come down at once the poor animal's throat vill be cut that werry night."

"Ha! – ha! – ha!" laughed the others.

"Vell, she sent four pound, and I put up with it," pursued Ginger; "but about a month arterwards she loses her favourite agin, and, strange to say, I finds it. The same game is played over again, and she comes down with another four pound. But she takes care this time that I sha'n't repeat the trick; for no sooner does she obtain persession of her favourite than she embarks in the steamer for France, in the hope of keeping her dog safe there."

"Oh! Miss Bailey, unfortinate Miss Bailey! – Fol de-riddle tol-ol-lol – unfortinate Miss Bailey!" sang the Tinker.

"But there's dog-fanciers in France, ain't there?" asked the Sandman.

"Lor, bless 'ee, yes," replied Ginger; "there's as many fanciers i' France as here. Vy, ve drives a smartish trade wi' them through them foreign steamers. There's scarcely a steamer as leaves the port o' London but takes out a cargo o' dogs. Ve sells 'em to the stewards, stokers, and sailors – cheap – and no questins asked. They goes to Ostend, Antverp, Rotterdam, Hamburg, and sometimes to Havre. There's a Mounseer Coqquilu as comes over to buy dogs, and ve takes 'em to him at a house near Billinsgit market."

"Then you're alvays sure o' a ready market somehow," observed the Sandman.

"Sartin, replied Ginger, "cos the law's so kind to us. Vy, bless you, a perliceman can't detain us, even if he knows ve've a stolen dog in our persession, and ve svears it's our own; and yet he'd stop you in a minnit if he seed you with a suspicious-lookin' bundle under your arm. Now, jist to show you the difference atwixt the two perfessions: – I steals a dog – walue, maybe, fifty pound, or p'raps more. Even if I'm catched i' the fact I may get fined twenty pound, or have six months' imprisonment; vile, if you steals an old fogle, walue three fardens, you'll get seven years abroad, to a dead certainty."

"That seems hard on us," observed the Sandman, reflectively.

"It's the law!" exclaimed Ginger, triumphantly. "Now, ve generally escapes by payin' the fine, 'cos our pals goes and steals more dogs to raise the money. Ve alvays stands by each other. There's a reg'lar horganisation among us; so ve can alvays bring vitnesses to svear vot ve likes, and ve so puzzles the beaks, that the case gets dismissed, and the constable says, 'Vich party shall I give the dog to, your vorship?' Upon vich, the beak replies, a-shakin of his vise noddle, 'Give it to the person in whose persession it was found. I have nuffin' more to do vith it.' In course the dog is delivered up to us."

"The law seems made for dog-fanciers," remarked the Tinker.

"Wot d'ye think o' this?" pursued Ginger. "I 'wos a-standin' at the corner o' Gray's Inn-lane vith some o' my pals near a coach-stand, ven a lady passes by vith this here dog – an' a beauty it is, a real long-eared Charley – a follerin' of her. Vell, the moment I spies it, I unties my apron, whips up the dog, and covers it up in a trice. Vell, the lady sees me, an' gives me in charge to a perliceman. But that si'nifies nuffin'. I brings six vitnesses to svear the dog vos mine, and I actually had it since it vos a blind little puppy; and, wot's more, I brings its mother, and that settles the pint. So in course I'm discharged; the dog is given up to me; and the lady goes avay lamentin'. I then plays the amiable, an' offers to sell it her for twenty guineas, seein' as how she had taken a fancy to it; but she von't bite. So if I don't sell it next week, I shall send it to Mounseer Coqquilu. The only vay you can go wrong is to steal a dog wi' a collar on, for if you do, you may get seven years' transportation for a bit o' leather and a brass plate vorth a shillin', vile the animal, though vorth a hundred pound, can't hurt you. There's law again – ha, ha!"

"Dog-fancier's law!" laughed the Sandman.

"Some of the Fancy is given to cruelty," pursued Ginger," and crops a dog's ears, or pulls out his teeth to disguise him; but I'm too fond o' the animal for that. I may frighten old ladies sometimes, as I told you afore, but I never seriously hurts their pets. Nor did I ever kill a dog for his skin, as some on 'em does."

"And you're always sure o' gettin' a dog, if you vants it, I s'pose?" inquired the Tinker.

"Alvays," replied Ginger. "No man's dog is safe. I don't care how he's kept, ve're sure to have him at last. Ve feels our vay with the sarvents, and finds out from them the walley the master or missis sets on the dog, and soon after that the animal's gone. Vith a bit o' liver, prepared in my partic'lar vay, I can tame the fiercest dog as ever barked, take him off his chain, an' bring him arter me at a gallop."

"And do respectable parties ever buy dogs knowin' they're stolen?" inquired the Tinker.

"Ay, to be sure," replied Ginger, "sometimes first-rate nobs. They put us up to it themselves; they'll say, 'I've jist left my Lord So-and-So's, and there I seed a couple o' the finest pointers I ever clapped eyes on. I vant you to get me list sich another couple.' Vell, ve understands in a minnit, an' in doo time the identicle dogs finds their vay to our customer."

"Oh! that's how it's done?" remarked the Sandman.

"Yes, that's the vay," replied Ginger. "Sometimes a party'll vant a couple o' dogs for the shootin' season; and then ve asks, 'Vich vay are you a-goin' – into Surrey or Kent?' And accordin' as the answer is given ve arranges our plans."

"Vell, yourn appears a profitable and safe employment, I must say," remarked the Sandman.

"Perfectly so," replied Ginger. "Nothin' can touch us till dogs is declared by statute to be property, and stealin' 'em a misdemeanour. And that won't occur in my time."

"Let's hope not," rejoined the other two.

"To come back to the pint from vich ve started," said the Tinker; "our gemman's case is not so surprisin' as it at first appears. There are some persons as believe they never will die – and I myself am of the same opinion. There's our old deputy here – him as ve calls Old Parr vy, he declares he lived in Queen Bess's time, recollects King Charles bein' beheaded perfectly vell, and remembers the Great Fire o' London, as if it only occurred yesterday."

"Walker!" exclaimed Ginger, putting his finger to his nose.

"You may larf, but it's true," replied the Tinker. "I recollect an old man tellin' me that he knew the deputy sixty years ago, and he looked jist the same then as now, – neither older nor younger."

44

"Humph !" exclaimed Ginger. "He don't look so old now."

"That's the cur'ousest part of it," said the Tinker. "He don't like to talk of his age unless you can get him i' the humour; but he once told me he didn't know why he lived so long, unless it were owin' to a potion he'd swallowed, vich his master, who was a great conjuror in Queen Bess's days, had brew'd."

"Pshaw!" exclaimed Ginger. "I thought you too knowin' a cove, Tinker, to be gulled by such an old-vife's story as that."

"Let's have the old fellow in and talk to him," replied the Tinker. "Here, lazy-bones," he added, rousing the sleeping youth, "go an' tell Old Parr ve vants his company over a glass o' rum-an'-vater."

III. The Hand and the Cloak

A furious barking from Mr. Ginger's dogs, shortly after the departure of the drowsy youth, announced the approach of a grotesque-looking little personage, whose shoulders barely reached to a level with the top of the table. This was Old Parr. The dwarf's head was much too large for his body, as is mostly the case with undersized persons, and was covered with a forest of rusty black hair, protected by a strangely shaped seal-skin cap. His hands and feet were equally disproportioned to his frame, and his arms were so long that he could touch his ankles while standing upright. His spine was crookened, and his head appeared buried in his breast. The general character of his face seemed to appertain to the middle period of life; but a closer inspection enabled the beholder to detect in it marks of extreme old age. The nose was broad and flat, like that of an orang-outang; the resemblance to which animal was heightened by a very long upper lip, projecting jaws, almost total absence of chin, and a retreating forehead. The little old man's complexion was dull and swarthy, but his eyes were keen and sparkling.

His attire was as singular as his person. Having recently served as double to a famous demon-dwarf at the Surrey Theatre, he had become possessed of a cast-off pair of tawny tights, an elastic shirt of the same material and complexion, to the arms of which little green bat-like wings were attached, while a blood-red tunic with vandyke points was girded round his waist. In this strange apparel his diminutive limbs were encased, while additional warmth was afforded by the great-coat already mentioned, the tails of which swept the floor after him like a train.

Having silenced his dogs with some difficulty, Mr. Ginger burst into a roar of laughter, excited by the little old man's grotesque appearance, in which he was joined by the Tinker; but the Sandman never relaxed a muscle of his sullen countenance.

Their hilarity, however, was suddenly checked by an inquiry from the dwarf, in a shrill, odd tone, 'whether they had sent for him only to laugh at him?'

"Sartainly not, deputy," replied the Tinker. "Here, lazy-bones, glasses o' rum-an'-vater, all round."

The drowsy youth bestirred himself to execute the command. The spirit was brought; water was procured from the boiling copper; and the Tinker handed his guest a smoking rummer, accompanied with a polite request to make himself comfortable.

Opposite the table at which the party were seated, it has been said, was a staircase old and crazy, and. but imperfectly protected by a broken hand-rail. Midway up it stood a door equally dilapidated, but secured by a chain and lock, of which Old Parr, as deputy-chamberlain, kept the key. Beyond this point, the staircase branched off on the right, and a row of stout wooden banisters, ranged like the feet of so many cattle, was visible from. beneath. Ultimately, the staircase reached a small gallery, if such a name can be applied to a narrow passage, communicating with the bedrooms, the doors of which, as a matter of needful precaution, were locked outside; and as the windows were grated, no one could leave his chamber without the knowledge of the landlord or his representative. No lights were allowed in the bedrooms, nor in the passage adjoining them.

Conciliated by the Tinker's offering, Old Parr mounted the staircase, and planting himself near the door, took off his great-coat, and sat down upon it. His impish garb being thus more fully displayed, he looked so unearthly and extraordinary that the dogs began to howl fearfully, and Ginger had enough to do to quiet them.

Silence being at length restored, the Tinker, winking slyly at his companions, opened the conversation.

"I say, deputy," he observed, "ve've bin havin' a bit o' a dispute vich you can settle for us."

"Well, let's see," squeaked the dwarf. "What is it?"

"Vy, it's relative to your age," rejoined the Tinker. "Ven wos you born?"

"It's so long ago, I can't recollect," returned Old Parr, rather sulkily.

"You must ha' seen some changes in your time?" resumed the Tinker, waiting till the little old man had made some progress with his grog.

"I rayther think I have – a few," replied Old Parr, whose tongue the generous liquid had loosened. "I've seen this great city of London pulled down, and built up again – if that's anything. I've seen it grow, and grow, till it has reached its present size. You'll scarcely believe me, when I tell you, that I recollect this Rookery of ours – this foul vagabond neighbourhood – an open country field, with hedges round it, and trees. And a lovely spot it was. Broad Saint Giles's, at the time I speak of, was a little country village, consisting of a few straggling houses standing by the roadside, and there wasn't a single habitation between it and Convent-garden (for so the present market was once called); while that garden, which was fenced round with pales, like a park, extended from Saint Martin's-lane to Drury-house, a great mansion situated on the easterly side of Drury-lane, amid a grove of beautiful timber."

"My eyes!" cried Ginger, with a prolonged whistle; "the place must be preciously transmogrified indeed!"

"If I were to describe the changes that have taken place in London since I've known It, I might go on talking for a month," pursued Old Parr. "The whole aspect of the place is altered. The Thames itself is unlike the Thames of old. Its waters were once as clear and bright above London-bridge as they are now at Kew or Richmond; and its banks, from Whitefriars to Scotland-yard, were edged with gardens. And then the thousand gay wherries and gilded barges that covered its bosom – all are gone – all are gone!"

"Those must ha' been nice times for the jolly young vatermen vich at Blackfriars wos used for to ply," chanted the Tinker; "but the steamers has put their noses out o' joint."

"True," replied Old Parr; "and I, for one, am sorry for it. Remembering, as I do, what the river used to be when enlightened by gay craft and merry company, I can't help wishing its waters less muddy, and those ugly coal-barges, lighters, and steamers, away. London is a mighty city, wonderful to behold and examine, inexhaustible in its wealth and power; but in point of beauty, it is not to be compared with the city of Queen Bess's days. You should have seen the Strand then – a line of noblemen's houses – and as to Lombard-street and Gracechurch-street, with their wealthy goldsmith's shops – but I don't like to think of 'em."

"Yell, I'm content vith Lunnun as it is," replied the Tinker, "'specially as there ain't much chance o' the ould city bein' rewived."

"Not much," replied the dwarf, finishing his glass, which was replenished at a sign from the Tinker.

"I s'pose, my wenerable, you've seen the king as bequeathed his name to these pretty creaters," said Ginger, raising his coat-pockets, so as to exhibit the heads of the two little black-and-tan spaniels.

"What! old Rowley?" cried the dwarf – "often. I was page to his favourite mistress, the Duchess of Cleveland, and I have seen him a hundred times with a pack of dogs of that description at his heels."

"Old Rowley wos a king arter my own 'art," said Ginger, rising and lighting a pipe at the fire. "He loved the femi-*nine* specious as well as the ca-*nine* specious. Can you tell us anythin' more about him?"

"Not now," replied Old Parr. "I've seen so much, and heard so much, that my brain is quite addled. My memory sometimes deserts me altogether, and my past life appears like a dream. Imagine what my feelings must be, to walk through streets, still called by the old names, but in other respects wholly changed. Oh! if you could but have a glimpse of Old London, you would not be able to endure the modern city. The very atmosphere was different from that which we now breathe, charged with the smoke of myriads of sea-coal fires; and the old picturesque houses had a charm about them, which the present habitations, however commodious, altogether want."

"You talk like one o' them smart chaps they calls, and werry properly, penny-a-liars," observed Ginger. "But you make me long to ha' lived i' those times."

"If you had lived in them, you would have belonged to Paris-garden, or the bull-baiting and bear-baiting houses in Southwark," replied Old Parr. "I've seen fellows just like you at each of those places. Strange, though times and fashions change, men continue the same. I often meet a face that I can remember in James the First's time. But the old places are gone – clean gone!"

"Accordin' to your own showin', my wenerable friend, you must ha' lived uppards o' two hundred and seventy year," said Ginger, assuming a consequential manner. "Now, doorin' all that time, have you never felt inclined to' kick the bucket?"

"Not the least," replied Old Parr. "My bodily health has been excellent. But, as I have just said, my intellects are a little impaired."

"Not a little, I should think," replied Ginger, hemming significantly. "I don't know vether you're a deceivin' of us or yourself, my wenerable; but von thing's quite clear – you can't have lived all that time. It's not in nater."

"Very well, then – I haven't," said Old Parr.

And he finished his rum-and-water, and set down the glass, which was instantly filled again by the drowsy youth.

"You've seen some picters o' Old Lunnum, and they've haanted you in your dreams, till you've begun to fancy you lived in those times," said Ginger.

"Very likely," replied Old Parr – "very likely."

There was something, however, in his manner calculated to pique the dog-fancier's curiosity.

"How comes it," he said, stretching out his legs, and arranging his neckcloth, – "how comes it, if you've lived so long, that you ain't higher up in the stirrups – better off, as folks say?"

The dwarf made no reply, but covering his face with his hands, seemed a prey to deep emotion. After a few moments' pause, Ginger repeated the question.

"If you won't believe what I tell you, it's useless to give an answer," said Old Parr, somewhat gruffly.

"Oh yes, I believe you, deputy," observed the Tinker, "and so does the Sandman."

"Well, then," replied the dwarf, "I'll tell you how it comes to pass. Fate has been against me. I've had plenty of chances, but I never could get on. I've been in a hundred different walks of life, but they always led down hill. It's my destiny."

"That's hard," rejoined the Tinker – "werry hard. But how d'ye account for livin' so long?" he added, winking as he spoke to the others.

"I've already given you an explanation," replied the dwarf.

"Ay, but it's a cur-ous story, and I vants my friends to hear it," said the Tinker, in a coaxing tone.

"Well then, to oblige you, I'll go through it again," rejoined the dwarf. "You must know I was for some time servant to Doctor Lamb, an old alchemist, who lived during the reign of good Queen Bess, and who used to pass all his time in trying to find out the secret of changing lead and copper into gold."

"I've known several indiwiduals as has found out that secret, wenerable," observed Ginger. "And ve calls 'em smashers, now-a-days not halchemists."

"Doctor Lamb's object was actually to turn base metal into gold," rejoined Old Parr, in a tone of slight contempt. "But his chief aim was to produce the Elixir of Long Life. Night and day he worked at the operation; – night and day I laboured with him, until at last we were both brought to the verge of the grave in our search after immortality. One night – I remember it well, – it was the last night of the sixteenth century, – a young man, severely wounded, was brought to my master's dwelling on London-bridge. I helped to convey him to the laboratory, where I left with the doctor, who was busy with his experiments. My curiosity being aroused, I listened at the door, and though I could not distinguish much that passed inside, I heard sufficient to convince me that Doctor Lamb had made the grand discovery, and succeeded in distilling the elixir. Having learnt this, I went down stairs, wondering what would next ensue. Half an hour elapsed, and while the bells were ringing in the new year joyfully, the young man whom I had assisted to carry upstairs, and whom I supposed at death's door, marched down as firmly as if nothing had happened, passed by me, and disappeared, before I could shake off my astonishment. I saw at once he had drunk the elixir."

"Ah! – ah!" exclaimed the Tinker, with a knowing glance at his companions, who returned it with gestures of equal significance.

"As soon as he was gone," pursued the dwarf, "I flew to the laboratory, and there, extended on the floor, I found the dead body of Dr. Lamb. I debated with myself what to do – whether to pursue his murderer, for such I accounted the young man; but, on reflection, I thought the course useless. I next looked round to see whether the precious elixir was gone. On the table stood a phial, from which a strong spirituous odour exhaled; but it was empty. I then turned my attention to a receiver, connected by a worm with an alembic on the furnace. On examining it, I found it contained a small quantity of a bright transparent liquid, which, poured forth into a glass, emitted precisely the same odour as the phial. Persuaded this must be the draught of immortality, I raised it to my lips; but apprehension lest it might be poison stayed my hand. Reassured, however, by the thought of the young man's miraculous recovery, I quaffed the potion. It was as if I had swallowed fire, and at first I thought all was over with me. I shrieked out; but there was no one to heed my cries, unless it were my dead master, and two or three skeletons with which the walls were garnished. And these, in truth, did seem to hear me; for the dead corpse opened its glassy orbs, and eyed me reproachfully; the skeletons shook their fleshless arms and gibbered; and the various strange objects with which the chamber was filled, seemed to deride and menace me. The terror occasioned by these fantasies, combined with the potency of the draught, took away my senses. When I recovered, I found all tranquil. Doctor Lamb was lying stark and stiff at my feet, with an expression of reproach on his fixed countenance; and the skeletons were hanging quietly in their places. Convinced that I was proof against death, I went forth. *But a curse went with me!* From that day to this, I have lived, but it has been in such poverty and distress, that I had better far have died. Besides, I am constantly haunted by visions of my old master. He seems to hold converse with me – to lead me into strange places."

"Exactly the case with the t'other," whispered the Tinker to the Sandman. "Have you ever, in the coorse o' your long life, met the young man as drank the 'lixir?" he inquired of the dwarf.

"Never."

"Do you happen to rekilect his name?"

"No; it has quite escaped my memory," answered Old Parr.

"Should you rekilect it, if you heerd it?" asked the Tinker.

"Perhaps I might," returned the dwarf; "but I can't say."

"Wos it Auriol Darcy?" demanded the other.

"That was the name," cried Old Parr, starting up in extreme surprise. "I heard Doctor Lamb call him so. But how, in the name of wonder, do you come to know it?"

"Ve've got summat, at last," said the Tinker, with a self-applauding glance at his friends.

"How do you come to know it, I say?" repeated the dwarf, in extreme agitation.

"Never mind," rejoined the Tinker, with a cunning look; "you see I does know some cur'ous matters as vell as you, my old file. You'll be good evidence, in case ve vishes to prove the fact agin him."

"Prove what? – and against whom?" cried the

"One more questin, and I've done," pursued the Tinker. "Should you know this young man again, in case you chanced to come across him?"

"No doubt of it," replied Old Parr; "his figure often flits before me in dreams."

"Shall ve let him into it?" said the Tinker, consulting his companions in a low tone.

"Ay – ay," replied the Sandman.

"Better vait a bit," remarked Ginger, shaking his head dubiously. "There's no hurry."

"No; ve must decide at vonce," said the Tinker. "Jist examine them papers," he added, handing the pocket-book to Old Parr, "and favour us vith your opinion on 'em."

The dwarf was about to unclasp the book committed to his charge, when a hand was suddenly thrust through the banisters of the upper part of the staircase, which, as has been already stated, was divided from the lower by the door. A piece of heavy black drapery next descended like a cloud, concealing all behind it except the hand, with which the dwarf was suddenly seized by the nape of the neck, lifted up in the air, and, notwithstanding his shrieks and struggles, carried clean off.

Great confusion attended his disappearance. The dogs set up a prodigious barking, and flew to the rescue – one of the largest of them passing over the body of the drowsy waiter, who had sought his customary couch upon the coals, and rousing him from his slumbers; while the Tinker, uttering a fierce imprecation, upset his chair in his haste to catch hold of the dwarf's legs; but the latter was already out of reach, and the next moment had vanished entirely.

'My eyes! here's a pretty go!" cried Ginger, who, with his back to the fire, had witnessed the occurrence in open-mouthed astonishment, "Vy, curse it! if the wenerable ain't a-taken the pocket-book with him! It's my opinion the devil has flown avay with the old feller. His time wos nearer at 'and than he expected."

"Devil or not, I'll have him back agin, or at all events the pocketbook!" cried the Tinker. And, dashing up the stairs, he caught hold of the railing above, and swinging himself up by a powerful effort, passed through an opening, occasioned by the removal of one of the banisters.

Groping along the gallery, which was buried in profound darkness, he shouted to the dwarf, but received no answer to his vociferations; neither could he discover any one, though he felt on either side of the passage with outstretched hands. The occupants of the different chambers, alarmed by the noise, called out to know what was going forward; but being locked in their rooms, they could render no assistance.

While the Tinker was thus pursuing his search in the dark, venting his rage and disappointment in the most dreadful imprecations, the staircase door was opened by the landlord, who had found the key in the great-coat left behind by the dwarf. With the landlord came the Sandman and Ginger, the latter of whom was attended by all his dogs, still barking furiously; while the rear of the party was brought up by the drowsy waiter, now wide awake with fright, and carrying a candle.

But though every nook and corner of the place was visited – though the attics were searched and all the windows examined – not a trace of the dwarf could be discovered, nor any clue to his mysterious disappearance detected. Astonishment and alarm sat on every countenance.

"What the devil can have become of him?" cried the landlord, with a look of dismay.

"Ay, that's the questin!" rejoined the Tinker. "I begin to be of Ginger's opinion, that the devil himself must have flown avay vith him. No von else could ha' taken a fancy to him."

"I only saw a hand and a black cloak," said the Sandman.

"I thought I seed a pair o' hoofs," cried the waiter; "and I'm quite sure I seed a pair o' great glitterin' eyes," he added, opening his own lacklustre orbs to their widest extent.

"It's a strange affair," observed the landlord, gravely. "It's certain that no one has entered the house wearing a cloak such as you describe; nor could any of the lodgers, to my knowledge, get out of their rooms. It was Old Parr's business, as you know, to lock 'em up carefully for the night."

"Veil, all's over vith him now," said the Tinker; "and vith our affair, too, I'm afeerd."

"Don't say die jist yet," rejoined Ginger. "The wenerable's gone, to be sure; and the only thing he has left behind him, barrin' his top-coat, is this here bit o' paper vich dropped out o' the pocket-book as he wos a-takin' flight, and vich I picked from the floor. It may be o' some use to us. But come, let's go down stairs. There's no good in stayin' here any longer."

Concurring in which sentiment, they all descended to the lower room.

IV. The Iron-Merchant's Daughter

A week had elapsed since Auriol Darcy was conveyed to the iron-merchant's dwelling, after the attack made upon him by the ruffians in the ruined house; and though almost recovered from the serious injuries he had received, he still remained the guest of his preserver.

It was a bright spring morning, when a door leading to the yard in front of the house opened, and a young girl, bright and fresh as the morning's self, issued from it.

A lovelier creature than Ebba Thorneycroft cannot be imagined. Her figure was perfection slight, tall, and ravishingly proportioned, with a slender waist, little limbs, and fairy feet that would have made the fortune of an opera-dancer. Her features were almost angelic in expression, with an outline of the utmost delicacy and precision not cold, classical regularity but that softer and incomparably more lovely mould peculiar to our own clime. Ebba's countenance was a type of Saxon beauty. Her complexion was pure white, tinged with a slight bloom. Her eyes were of a serene summer blue, arched over by brows some shades darker than the radiant tresses that fell on either cheek, and were parted over a brow smoother than alabaster. Her attire was simple, but tasteful, and by its dark colour threw into relief the exceeding fairness of her skin.

Ebba's first care was to feed her favourite linnet, placed in a cage over the door. Having next patted the head of a huge bulldog who came out of his kennel to greet her, and exchanged a few words with two men employed at a forge in the inner part of the building on the right, she advanced farther into the yard.

This part of the premises, being strewn with ironwork of every possible shape, presented a very singular appearance, and may merit some description. There were heaps of rusty iron chains flung together like fishermen's nets, old iron area-guards, iron kitchen-fenders, old grates, safes, piles of old iron bowls, a large assortment of old iron pans and dishes, a ditto of old ovens, kettles without number, sledge-hammers, anvils, braziers, chimney-cowls, and smokejacks.

Stout upright posts, supporting cross-beams on the top, were placed at intervals on either side of the yard, and these were decorated, in the most artistic style, with rat-traps, man-traps, iron lanterns, pulleys, padlocks, chains, trivets, triangles, iron rods, disused street lamps, dismounted cannon and anchors. Attached to hooks in the cross-beam nearest the house hung a row of old horseshoes, while from the centre depended a large rusty bell. Near the dog's kennel was a tool-box, likewise garnished with horse-shoes, and containing pincers, files, hammers, and other implements proper to the smith. Beyond this was an open doorway leading to the workshop, where the two men before mentioned were busy at the forge;.

Though it was still early, the road was astir with passengers, and many wagons and carts, laden with hay, straw, and vegetables, were passing. Ebba, however, had been solely drawn forth by the beauty of the morning, and she stopped for a moment at the street gate, to breathe the barmy air. As she inhaled the gentle breeze, and felt the warm sunshine upon her cheek, her thoughts wandered away into the green meadows in which she had strayed as a child, and she longed to ramble amid them again. Perhaps she scarcely desired a solitary stroll; but however this might be, she was too much engrossed by the reverie to notice a tall man, wrapped in a long black cloak, who regarded her with the most fixed attention, as he passed on the opposite side of the road.

Proceeding to a short distance, this personage crossed over, and returned slowly towards the iron-merchant's dwelling. Ebba then, for the first time, remarked him, and was startled by his strange, sinister appearance. His features were handsome, but so malignant and fierce in expression, that they inspired only aversion. A sardonic grin curled his thin lips, and his short, crisply curled hair, raven black in hue, contrasted forcibly and disagreeably with his cadaverous complexion. An attraction like that of the snake seemed to reside in his dark blazing eyes, for Ebba trembled like a bird beneath their influence, and could not remove her gaze from them. A vague presentiment of coming ill smote her, and she dreaded lest the mysterious being before her might be connected in some inexplicable way with her future destiny.

On his part, the stranger was not insensible to the impression he had produced, and suddenly halting, he kept his eyes riveted on those of the girl, who, after remaining spell-bound, as it were, for a few moments, precipitately retreated towards the house.

Just as she reached the door, and was about to pass through it, Auriol came forth. He was pale, as if from recent suffering, and bore his left arm in a sling.

"You look agitated," he said, noticing Ebba's uneasiness. "What has happened?"

"Not much," she replied, a deep blush mantling her cheeks. "But I have been somewhat alarmed by the person near the gate."

"Indeed!" cried Auriol, darting forward. "Where is he? I see no one."

"Not a tall man, wrapped in a long black cloak?" rejoined Ebba, following him cautiously. "Ha!" cried Auriol. "Has he been here?"

"Then you know the person I allude to?" she rejoined.

"I know some one answering his description," he replied, with a forced smile.

"Once beheld, the man I mean is not to be forgotten," said Ebba. "He has a countenance such as I never saw before. If I could believe in the 'evil eye', I should be sure he possessed it."

58

"'Tis he, there can be no doubt," rejoined Auriol, in a sombre tone.

"Who and what is he, then?" demanded Ebba.

"He is a messenger of ill," replied Auriol, "and I am thankful he is gone."

"Are you quite sure of it?" she asked, glancing timorously up and down the road. But the mysterious individual could no longer be seen.

"And so, after exciting my curiosity in this manner, you will not satisfy it?" she said.

"I cannot," rejoined Auriol, somewhat sternly.

"Nay, then, since you are so ungracious, I shall go and prepare breakfast," she replied. "My father must be down by this time."

"Stay!" cried Auriol, arresting her, as she was about to pass through the door. "I wish to have a word with you."

Ebba stopped, and the bloom suddenly forsook her cheeks.

But Auriol seemed unable to proceed. Neither dared to regard the other; and a profound silence prevailed between them for a few moments.

"Ebba," said Auriol at length, "I am about to leave your father's house today."

"Why so soon?" she exclaimed, looking up into his face. "You are not entirely recovered yet."

"I dare not stay longer," he said.

"Dare not!" cried Ebba. And she again cast down her eyes; but Auriol made no reply.

Fortunately the silence was broken by the clinking of the smith's hammers upon the anvil. "If you must really go," said Ebba, looking up, after a long pause, "I hope we shall see you again?"

"Most assuredly," replied Auriol. "I owe your worthy father a deep debt of gratitude – a debt which, I fear, I shall never be able to repay."

"My father is more than repaid in saving your life," she replied. "I am sure he will be sorry to learn you are going so soon."

"I have been here a week," said Auriol. "If I remained longer, I might not be able to go at all."

There was another pause, during which a stout old fellow in the workshop quitted the anvil for a moment, and, catching a glimpse of the young couple, muttered to his helpmate:

"I say, Ned, I'm a-thinkin' our master'll soon have a son-in-law. There's pretty plain signs on it at yonder door."

"So there be, John," replied Ned, peeping round. "He's a good-lookin' young feller that. I wish ve could hear their discoorse."

"No, that ain't fair," replied John, raking some small coal upon the fire, and working away at the bellows.

"I would not for the world ask a disagreeable question," said Ebba, again raising her eyes, "but since you are about to quit us, I must confess I should like to know something of your history."

"Forgive me if I decline to comply with your desire," replied Auriol. "You would not believe me, were I to relate my history. But this I may say, that it is stranger and wilder than any you ever heard. The prisoner, in his cell is not restrained by more terrible fetters than those which bind me to silence."

Ebba gazed at him as if she feared his reasoning were wandering.

"You think me mad," said Auriol; "would I were so! But I shall never lose the clear perception of my woes. Hear me, Ebba! Fate has brought me into this house. I have seen you, and experienced your gentle ministry; and it is impossible, so circumstanced, to be blind to your attractions. I have only been too sensible to them – but I will not dwell on that theme, nor run the risk of exciting a passion which must destroy you. I will ask you to hate me – to regard me as a monster whom you ought to shun rather than as a being for whom you should entertain the slightest sympathy."

"You have some motive in saying this to me," cried the terrified girl.

"My motive is to warn you," said Auriol. "If you love me, you are lost – utterly lost!"

She was so startled, that she could make no reply, but burst into tears. Auriol took her hand, which she unresistingly yielded.

"A terrible fatality attaches to me, in which you must have no share," he said, in a solemn tone.

"Would you had never come to my father's house!" she exclaimed, in a voice of anguish.

"Is it, then, too late?" cried Auriol, despairingly.

"It is – if to love you be fatal," she rejoined.

"Ha!" exclaimed Auriol, striking his forehead with his clenched hand. "Recall your words – Ebba – recall them – but no, once uttered – it is impossible. You are bound to me for ever. I must fulfil my destiny."

At this juncture a low growl broke from the dog, and, guided by the sound, the youthful couple beheld, standing near the gate, the tall dark man in the black cloak. A fiendish smile sat upon his countenance.

"That is the man who frightened me!" cried Ebba.

"It is the person I supposed!" ejaculated Auriol. "I must speak to him. Leave me, Ebba. I will join you presently."

And as the girl, half sinking with apprehension, withdrew, he advanced quickly toward the intruder.

"I have sought you for some days," said the tall man, in a stern, commanding voice. "You have not kept your appointment with me."

"I could not," replied Auriol – "an accident has befallen me."

"I know it," rejoined the other. "I am aware you were assailed by ruffians in the ruined house over the way. But you are recovered now, and can go forth. You ought to have communicated with me."

"It was my intention to do so," said Auriol.

"Our meeting cannot be delayed much longer," pursued the stranger. "I will give you three more days. On the evening of the last day, at the hour of seven, I shall look for you at the foot of the statue in Hyde Park."

"I will be there," replied Auriol.

"That girl must be the next victim," said the stranger, with a grim smile.

"Peace!" thundered Auriol.

"Nay, I need not remind you of the tenure by which you maintain your power," rejoined the stranger. "But I will not trouble you further now."

And, wrapping his cloak more closely round him, he disappeared.

"Fate has once more involved me in its net," cried Auriol, bitterly. "But I will save Ebba, whatever it may cost me. I will see her no more."

And instead of returning to the house, he hurried away in the opposite direction of the stranger.

V. The Meeting Near the Statue

The evening of the third day arrived, and Auriol entered Hyde Park by Stanhope-gate. Glancing at his watch, and finding it wanted nearly three quarters of an hour of the time appointed for his meeting with the mysterious stranger, he struck across the Park, in the direction of the Serpentine River. Apparently he was now perfectly recovered, for his arm was without the support of the sling, and he walked with great swiftness. But his countenance was deathly pale, and his looks were so wild and disordered, that the few persons he encountered shrank from him aghast.

A few minutes' rapid walking brought him to the eastern extremity of the Serpentine, and advancing close to the edge of the embankment, he gazed at the waters beneath his feet.

"I would plunge into them, if I could find repose," he murmured. "But it would avail nothing. I should only add to my sufferings. No; I must continue to endure the weight of a life burned by crime and remorse, till I can find out the means of freeing myself from it. Once I dreaded this unknown danger, but now I seek for it in vain."

The current of his thoughts were here interrupted by the sudden appearance of a dark object on the surface of the water, which he at first took to he a huge fish, with a pair of green fins springing from its back; but after watching it more closely for a few moments, he became convinced that it was a human being, tricked out in some masquerade attire, while the slight struggles which it made proved that life was not entirely extinct.

Though, the moment before, he had contemplated self-destruction, and had only been restrained from the attempt by the certainty of failing in his purpose, instinct prompted him to rescue the perishing creature before him. Without hesitation, therefore, and without tarrying to divest himself of his clothes, he dashed into the water, and striking out, instantly reached the object of his quest, which still continued to float, and turning it over, for the face was downwards, he perceived it was an old man, of exceedingly small size, habited in a pantomimic garb. He also remarked that a rope was twisted round the neck of the unfortunate being, making it evident that some violent attempt had been made upon his life.

Without pausing for further investigation, he took firm hold of the leathern wings of the dwarf, and with his disengaged hand propelled himself towards the shore, dragging the other after him. The next instant he reached the bank, clambered up the low brickwork, and placed his burden in safety.

The noise of the plunge had attracted attention, and several persons now hurried to the spot. On coming up, and finding Auriol bending over a water-sprite – for such, at first sight, the dwarf appeared – they could not repress their astonishment. Wholly insensible to the presence of those around him, Auriol endeavoured to recall where he had seen the dwarf before. All at once, the recollection flashed upon him, and he cried aloud, "Why, it is my poor murdered grandfather's attendant, Flapdragon! But no no! - he must be dead ages ago! Yet the resemblance is singularly striking!"

Auriol's exclamations, coupled with his wild demeanour, surprised the bystanders, and they came to the conclusion that he must be a travelling showman, who had attempted to drown his dwarf – the grotesque, impish garb of the latter convincing them that he had been exhibited at a booth. They made signs, therefore, to each other not to let Auriol escape, and one of them, raising the dwarf's head on his knee, produced a flask, and poured some brandy from it down his throat, while others chafed his hands These efforts were attended with much speedier success than might have been anticipated. After a struggle or two for respiration the dwarf opened his eyes, and gazed at the group around him.

"It must be Flapdragon!" exclaimed Auriol.

"Ah! who calls me?" cried the dwarf.

"I!" rejoined Auriol. "Do you not recollect me?"

"To be sure!" exclaimed the dwarf, gazing at him fixedly; "you are – " and he stopped.

"You have been thrown into the water, Master Flapdragon?" cried a bystander, noticing the cord round the dwarf's throat.

"I have," replied the little old man.

"By your governor – that is, by this person?" cried another, laying hold of Auriol.

"By him – no," said the dwarf; "I have not seen that gentleman for nearly three centuries."

"Three centuries, my little patriarch?" said the man who had given him the brandy. "That's a long time. Think again."

"It's perfectly true, nevertheless," replied the dwarf.

"His wits have been washed away by the water," said the first speaker. "Give him a drop more brandy."

"Not a bit of it," rejoined the dwarf; "my senses were never clearer than at this moment. At last we have met," he continued, addressing Auriol, "and I hope we shall not speedily part again. We hold life by the same tie."

"How came you in the desperate condition in which I found you?" demanded Auriol, evasively.

"I was thrown into the canal with a stone to my neck, like a dog about to be drowned," replied the dwarf. "But, as you are aware, I'm not so easily disposed of."

Again the bystanders exchanged significant looks.

"By whom was the attempt made?" inquired Auriol.

"I don't know the villain's name," rejoined the dwarf, "but he's a very tall, dark man, and is generally wrapped in a long black cloak."

"Ha!" exclaimed Auriol. "When was it done?"

"Some nights ago, I should fancy," replied the dwarf, "for I've been a terrible long time under water. I have only just managed to shake off the stone."

At this speech there was a titter of incredulity among the bystanders.

"You may laugh, but it's true!" cried the dwarf, angrily.

"We must speak of this anon, said Auriol. "Will you convey him to the nearest tavern?" he added, placing money in the hands of the man who held the dwarf in his arms.

"Willingly, sir," replied the man. "I'll take him to the Life Guardsman, near the barracks, that's the nearest public."

"I'll join him there in an hour," replied Auriol, moving away.

And as he disappeared, the man took up his little burden, and bent his steps towards the barracks.

Utterly disregarding the dripping state of his habiliments, Auriol proceeded quickly to the place of rendezvous. Arrived there, he looked around, and not seeing any one, flung himself upon a bench at the foot of the gentle eminence on which the gigantic statue of Achilles is placed.

It was becoming rapidly dark, and heavy clouds, portending speedy rain, increased the gloom. Auriol's thoughts were sombre as the weather and the hour, and he fell into a deep fit of abstraction, from which he was roused by a hand laid on his shoulder.

Recoiling at the touch, he raised his eyes, and beheld the stranger leaning over him, and gazing at him with a look of diabolical exultation. The cloak was thrown partly aside, so as to display the tall, gaunt figure of its wearer; while the large collar of sable fur with which it was decorated stood out like the wings of a demon. The stranger's hat was off, and his high broad forehead, white as marble, was fully revealed.

"Our meeting must be brief," he said. "Are you prepared to fulfil the compact?"

"What do you require?" replied Auriol.

"Possession of the girl I saw three days ago," said the other; "the iron-merchant's daughter, Ebba. She must be mine."

"Never!" cried Auriol, firmly – "never!"

"Beware how you tempt me to exert my power," said the stranger; "she *must* be mine – or –"

"I defy you!" rejoined Auriol; "I will never consent."

"Fool!" cried the other, seizing him by the arm, and fixing a withering glance upon him. "Bring her to me ere the week be out, or dread my vengeance!"

And, enveloping himself in his cloak, he retreated behind the statue, and was lost to view.

As he disappeared, a moaning wind arose, and heavy rain descended. Still Auriol did not quit the bench.

Intermean

I. The Tomb of the Rosicrucian

On the night of the 1st of March, 1800, and at a late hour, a man, wrapped in a large horseman's cloak, and of strange and sinister appearance, entered an old deserted house in the neighbourhood of Stepney-green. He was tall, carried himself very erect, and seemed in the full vigour of early manhood; but his features had a worn and ghastly look, as if bearing the stamp of long-indulged and frightful excesses, while his dark gleaming eyes gave him an expression almost diabolical.

This person had gained the house from a garden behind it, and now stood in a large dismantled hall, from which a broad oaken staircase, with curiously-carved banisters, led to a gallery, and hence to the upper chambers of the habitation. Nothing could be more dreary than the aspect of the place. The richly moulded ceiling was festooned with spiders' webs, and in some places had fallen in heaps upon the floor; the glories of the tapestry upon the walls were obliterated by damps; the squares and black and white marble, with which the hall was paved, were loosened, and quaked beneath the footsteps; the wide and empty fireplace yawned like the mouth of a cavern; the bolts of the closed windows were rusted in their sockets; and the heaps of dust before the outer door proved that long years had elapsed since any one had passed through it.

Taking a dark lantern from beneath his cloak, the individual in question gazed for a moment around him, and then, with a sardonic smile playing upon his features, directed his steps towards a room on the right, the door of which stood open.

This chamber, which was large and cased with oak, was wholly unfurnished, like the hall, and in an equally dilapidated condition. The only decoration remaining on its walls was the portrait of a venerable personage in the cap and gown of Henry the Eighth's time, painted against a panel–a circumstance which had probably saved it from destruction and beneath it, fixed in another panel, a plate of brass,

68

covered with mystical characters and symbols, and inscribed with the name Cyprianus de Rougemont, Fra. R.C. The same name likewise appeared upon a label beneath the portrait, with the date, 1550.

Pausing before the portrait, the young man threw the light of the lantern full upon it, and revealed features somewhat resembling his own in form, but of a severe and philosophic cast. In the eyes alone could be discerned the peculiar and terrible glimmer which distinguished his own glances. After regarding the portrait for some time fixedly, he thus addressed it:

"Dost hear me, old ancestor?" he cried. "I, thy descendant, Cyprian de Rougemont, call upon thee to point out where thy gold is hidden? I know that thou wert a brother of the Rosy Cross—one of the illuminati–and didst penetrate the mysteries of nature, and enter the region of light. I know also, that thou wert buried in this house with a vast treasure; but though I have made diligent search for it, and others have searched before me, thy grave has never yet been discovered! Listen to me! Methought Satan appeared to me in a dream last night, and bade me come hither, and I should find what I sought. The conditions he proposed were, that I should either give him my own soul, or win him that of Auriol Darcy. I assented. I am here. Where is thy treasure?"

After a pause, he struck the portrait with his clenched hand, exclaiming in a loud voice:

"Dost hear me, I say, old ancestor? I call on thee to give me thy treasure. Dost hear, I say?"

And he repeated the blow with greater violence.

Disturbed by the shock, the brass plate beneath the picture started from its place, and fell to the ground.

"What is this?" cried Rougemont, gazing into the aperture left by the plate. "Ha!–my invocation has been heard!"

And, snatching up the lantern, he discovered, at the bottom of a little recess, about two feet deep, a stone, with an iron ring in the centre of it. Uttering a joyful cry, he seized the ring, and drew the stone forward without difficulty, disclosing an open space beyond it.

"This, then,' is the entrance to my ancestor's tomb," cried Rougemont; "there can be no doubt of it. The old Rosicrucian has kept his secret well; but the devil has helped me to wrest it from him. And now to procure the necessary implements, in case, as is not unlikely, I should experience further difficulty."

With this, he hastily quitted the room, but returned almost immediately with a mallet, a lever, and a pitchfork; armed with which and the lantern, he crept through the aperture. This done, he found himself at the head of a stone staircase, which he descended, and came to the arched entrance of a vault. The door, which was of stout oak, was locked, but holding up the light towards it, he read the following inscription:

POST C.C.L. ANNOS PATEBO, 1550.

"In two hundred and fifty years I shall open!" cried Rougemont, "and the date 1550–why, the exact time is arrived. Old Cyprian must have foreseen what would happen, and evidently intended to make me his heir. There was no occasion for the devil's interference. And see, the key is in the lock. So!" And he turned it, and pushing against the door with some force, the rusty hinges gave way, and it fell inwards.

From the aperture left by the fallen door, a soft and silvery light, streamed forth, and, stepping forward, Rougemont found himself in a spacious vault, from the ceiling of which hung a large globe of crystal, containing in its heart a little flame, which diffused a radiance gentle as that of the moon, around, This, then, was the ever-burning lamp of the Rosicrucians, and Rougemont gazed at if with astonishment. Two hundred and fifty years had elapsed since that wondrous flame had been lighted, and yet it burnt on brightly as ever. Hooped round the globe was a serpent with its tail in its mouth–an emblem of eternity–wrought in purest gold; while above it were a pair of silver wings, in

70

allusion to the soul. Massive chains of the more costly metal, fashioned like twisted snakes, served as suspenders to the lamp.

But Rougemont's astonishment at this marvel quickly gave way to other feelings, and he gazed around the vault with greedy eyes.

It was a septilateral chamber, about eight feet high built of stone, and supported by beautifully groined arches. The surface of the masonry was as smooth and fresh as if the chisel had only just left it.

In six of the corners were placed large chests, ornamented with ironwork of the most exquisite workmanship, and these Rougemont's imagination pictured as filled with inexhaustible treasure; while in the seventh corner, near the door, was a beautiful little piece of monumental sculpture in white marble, representing two kneeling and hooded figures, holding a veil between them, which partly concealed the entrance to a small recess. On one of the chests opposite the monument just described stood a strangely formed bottle and a cup of antique workmanship, both incrusted with gems.

The walls were covered with circles, squares and diagrams, and in some places were ornamented with grotesque carvings. In the centre of the vault was a round altar of black marble, covered with a plate of gold, on which Rougemont read the following inscription:

Hoc universi compendium unius mihi sepulcrum feci.

"Here, then, old Cyprian lies," he cried.

And, prompted by some irresistible impulse, he seized the altar by the upper rim, and overthrew it. The heavy mass of marble fell with a thundering crash, breaking asunder the flag beneath it. It might be the reverberation of the vaulted roof, but a deep groan seemed to reproach the young man for his sacrilege. Undeterred, however, by this warning, Rougemont placed the point of the lever between the interstices of the broken stone, and, exerting all his strength, speedily raised the fragments, and laid open the grave.

Within it, in the garb he wore in life, with his white beard streaming to his waist, lay the unconfined body of his ancestor, Cyprian de Rougemont. The corpse had evidently been carefully embalmed, and the features were unchanged by decay. Upon the breast, with the hands placed over it, lay a large book, bound in black vellum, and fastened with brazen clasps. Instantly possessing himself of this mysterious looking volume, Rougemont knelt upon the nearest chest, and opened it. But he was disappointed in his expectation. All the pages he examined were filled with cabalistic characters, which he was totally unable to decipher.

At length, however, he chanced upon One page, the import of which he comprehended, and he remained for some time absorbed in its contemplation, while an almost fiendish smile played upon his features.

"Aha!" he exclaimed, closing the volume, "I see now the cause of my extraordinary dream. My ancestor's wondrous power was of infernal origin–the result, in fact, of a compact with the Prince of Darkness. But what care I for that? Give me wealth–no matter what source it comes from!–ha! ha!"

And seizing the lever, he broke open the chest beside him. It was filled with bars of silver. The next he visited in the same way was full of gold. The third was laden with pearls and precious stones; and the rest contained treasure to an incalculable amount. Rougemont gazed at them in transports of joy.

"At length I have my wish," he cried. "Boundless wealth, and therefore boundless power is mine. I can riot in pleasure–riot in vengeance. As to my soul, I will run the risk of its perdition; but it shall go hard if I destroy not that of Auriol. His love of play and his passion for Edith Talbot shall be the means by which I will work. But I must not neglect another agent which is offered me. That bottle, I have learnt from yon volume, contains an infernal potion, which, without destroying life, shatters the brain, and creates maddening fancies. It will well serve my purpose; and I thank thee, Satan, for the gift."

II. The Compact

Another two months after this occurrence, and near midnight, a young man was hurrying along Pall-mall, with a look of the wildest despair, when his headlong course was suddenly arrested by a strong grasp, while a familiar voice sounded in his ear.

"It is useless to meditate self-destruction Auriol Darcy," cried the person who had checked him. "If you find life a burden, I can make it tolerable to you."

Turning round at the appeal, Auriol beheld a tall man, wrapped in a long black cloak, whose sinister features were well known to him.

"Leave me, Rougemont!" he cried, fiercely. "I want no society— above all, not yours. You know very well that you have ruined me, and that nothing more is to be got from me. Leave me, I say, or I may do you a mischief."

"Tut, tut, Auriol, I am your friend!" replied Rougemont. "I purpose to relieve your distress." "Will you give me back the money you have won from me?" cried Auriol. "Will you pay my inexorable creditors? Will you save me from a prison?"

"I will do all this, and more," replied Rougemont. "I will make you one of the richest men in London."

"Spare your insulting jests, sir," cried Auriol. "I am in no mood to bear them."

"I am not jesting," rejoined Rougemont. "Come with me, and you shall be convinced of my sincerity."

Auriol at length assented, and they turned into Saint James's-square, and paused before a magnificent house. Rougemont ascended the steps. Auriol, who had accompanied him almost mechanically, gazed at him with astonishment.

"Do you live here?" he inquired.

"Ask no questions," replied Rougemont, knocking at the door, which was instantly opened by a hall porter, while other servants in rich liveries appeared at a distance. Rougemont addressed a few words in an undertone to them, and they instantly bowed respectfully to Auriol, while the foremost of them led the way up a magnificent staircase.

All this was a mystery to the young man, but he followed his conductor without a word, and was presently ushered into a gorgeously furnished and brilliantly illuminated apartment.

The servant then left them; and as soon as he was gone Auriol exclaimed–"Is it to mock me that you have brought me hither?"

"To mock you–no," replied Rougemont. "I have told you that I mean to make you rich. But you look greatly exhausted. A glass of wine will revive you."

And as he spoke, he stepped towards a small cabinet, and took from it a curiously-shaped bottle and a goblet.

"Taste this wine–it has been long in our family," he added, filling the cup.

"It is a strange, bewildering drink," cried Auriol, setting down the empty goblet, and passing his hand before his eyes.

"You have taken it upon an empty stomach–that is all," said Rougemont. "You will be better anon."

"I feel as if I were going mad," cried Auriol. "It is some damnable potion you have given me."

"Ha! ha!" laughed Rougemont. "It reminds you of the elixir you once quaffed–eh?"

"A truce to this raillery!" cried Auriol, angrily. "I have said I am in no mood to bear it!"

74

"Pshaw! I mean no offence," rejoined the other, changing his manner. "What think you of this house?"

"That it is magnificent," replied Auriol, gazing around. "I envy you its possession."

"It shall be yours, if you please," replied Rougemont.

"Mine! you are mocking me again."

"Not in the least. You shall buy it from me, if you please.'"

"At what price?" asked Auriol, bitterly.

"At a price you can easily pay," replied the other. "Come this way, and we will conclude the bargain."

Proceeding towards the farther end of the room, they entered a small exquisitely furnished chamber, surrounded with sofas of the most luxurious description. In the midst was a table, on which writing materials were placed.

"It were a fruitless boon to give you this house without the means of living in it," said Rougemont, carefully closing the door. "This pocket-book will furnish you with them."

"Notes to an immense amount!" cried Auriol, opening the pocket-book, and glancing at its contents.

"They are yours, together with the house," cried Rougemont, "if you will but sign a compact with me."

"A compact!" cried Auriol, regarding him with a look of undefinable terror. "Who and what are you?"

"Some men would call me the devil!" replied Rougemont, carelessly. "But you know me too well to suppose that I merit such a designation. I offer you wealth. What more could you require?"

"But upon what terms?" demanded Auriol.

"The easiest imaginable," replied the other. "You shall judge for yourself."

And as he spoke, he opened a writing-desk upon the table, and took from it a parchment.

"Sit down," he added, "and read this."

Auriol complied, and as he scanned the writing he became transfixed with fear and astonishment, while the pocket-book dropped from his grasp.

After a while, he looked up at Rougemont, who was leaning over his shoulder, and whose features were wrinkled with a derisive smile.

"Then you are the Fiend?" he cried.

"If you will have it so—certainly," replied the other.

"You are Satan in the form of the man I once knew," cried Auriol. "Avaunt! I will have no dealings with you."

"I thought you wiser than to indulge in such idle fears, Darcy," rejoined the other. "Granting even your silly notion of me to be correct, what need you be alarmed? You are immortal."

"True," rejoined Auriol thoughtfully; "but yet—"

"Pshaw!" rejoined the other, "sign and have done with the matter."

"By this compact I am bound to deliver a victim—a female victim—whenever you shall require it," cried Auriol.

"Precisely," replied the other; "you can have no difficulty in fulfilling that condition."

"But if I fail in doing so, I am doomed—"

"But you will not fail," interrupted the other, lighting a taper, and sealing the parchment. "Now sign it."

Auriol mechanically took the pen, and gazed fixedly on the document.

"I shall bring eternal destruction on myself if I sign it," he muttered.

"A stroke of the pen will rescue you from utter ruin," said Rougemont, leaning over his shoulder. "Riches and happiness are yours. You will not have such another chance."

"Tempter!" cried Auriol, hastily attaching his signature to the paper. But he instantly started back aghast at the fiendish laugh that rang in his ears.

"I repent–give it me back!" he cried, endeavouring to snatch the parchment which Rougemont thrust into his bosom.

"It is too late!" cried the latter, in a triumphant tone. "You are mine–irredeemably mine."

"Ha!" exclaimed Auriol, sinking back on the couch.

"I leave you in possession of your house," pursued Rougemont; "but I shall return in a week, when I shall require my first victim."

"Your first victim! oh, Heaven!" exclaimed Auriol.

"Ay, and my choice falls on Edith Talbot!" replied Rougemont.

"Edith Talbot!" exclaimed Auriol; "she your victim! Think you I would resign her I love better than life to you?"

"It is because she loves you that I have chosen her," rejoined Rougemont, with a bitter laugh. "And such will ever be the case with you. Seek not to love again, for your passion will be fatal to the object of it. When the week has elapsed, I shall require Edith at your hands. Till then, farewell!"

"Stay!" cried Auriol. "I break the bargain with thee, fiend. I will have none of it. I abjure thee."

And he rushed wildly after Rougemont, who had already gained the larger chamber; but, ere he could reach him, the mysterious individual had passed through the outer door, and when Auriol emerged upon the gallery, he was nowhere to be seen.

Several servants immediately answered the frantic shouts of the young man, and informed him that Mr. Rougemont had quitted the house some moments ago, telling them that their master was perfectly satisfied with the arrangements he had made for him.

"And we hope nothing has occurred to alter your opinion, sir?" said the hall porter.

"You are sure Mr. Rougemont is gone?" cried Auriol.

"Oh, quite sure, sir," cried the hall porter. "I helped him on with his cloak myself. He said he should return this day week."

"If he comes I will not see him," cried Auriol, sharply; "mind that. Deny me to him; and on no account whatever let him enter the house."

"Your orders shall be strictly obeyed," replied the porter, staring with surprise.

"Now leave me," cried Auriol.

And as they quitted him, he added, in a tone and with a gesture of the deepest despair, "All precautions are useless. I am indeed lost!"

III. Irresolution

On returning to the cabinet, where his fatal compact with Rougemont had been signed, Auriol perceived the pocket-book lying on the floor near the table, and, taking it up, he was about to deposit it in the writing-desk, when an irresistible impulse prompted him once more to examine its contents. Unfolding the roll of notes, he counted them, and found they amounted to more than a hundred thousand pounds. The sight of so much wealth, and the thought of the pleasure and the power it would procure him, gradually dispelled his fears, and arising in a transport of delight, he exclaimed–"Yes, yes–all obstacles are now removed! When Mr. Talbot finds I am become thus wealthy, he will no longer refuse me his daughter. But I am mad," he added, suddenly checking himself–"worse than mad, to indulge such hopes. If it be indeed the Fiend to whom I have sold myself, I have no help from perdition! if it be man, I am scarcely less terribly fettered. In either case, I will not, remain here longer; nor will I avail myself of this ac-cursed money, which has tempted me to my undoing."

And, hurling the pocket-book to the farther end of the room, he was about to pass through the door, when a mocking laugh arrested him. He looked round with astonishment and dread, but could see no one. After a while, he again moved forward, but a voice, which he rec-ognised as that of Rougemont, called upon him to stay.

"It will be in vain to fly," said the unseen speaker. "You cannot escape me. Whether you remain here or not–whether you use the wealth I have given you, or leave it behind you–you cannot annul your bargain. With this knowledge, you are at liberty to go. But remember, on the seventh night from this I shall require Edith Talbot from you!"

"Where are you fiend?" demanded Auriol, gazing around, furi-ously. "Show yourself, that I may confront you."

A mocking laugh was the only response deigned to this injunc-tion.

"Give me back the compact," cried Auriol, imploringly. "It was signed in ignorance. I knew not the price I was to pay for your assistance. Wealth is of no value to me without Edith."

"Without wealth you could not obtain her," replied the voice. "You are only, therefore, where you were. But you will think better of the bargain tomorrow. Meanwhile, I counsel you to place the money you have so unwisely cast from you safely under lock and key, and to seek repose. You will awaken with very different thoughts in the morning."

"How am I to account for my sudden accession of wealth?" inquired Auriol, after a pause.

"You a gambler, and ask that question!" returned the unseen stranger with a bitter laugh. "But I will make your mind easy on that score. As regards the house, you will find a regular conveyance of it within that writing-desk, while the note lying on the table, which bears your address, comes from me, and announces the payment of a hundred and twenty thousand pounds to you, as a debt of honour. You see I have provided against every difficulty. And now farewell!"

The voice was then hushed; and though Auriol addressed several other questions to the unseen speaker no answer was returned him.

After some moments of irresolution, Auriol once more took up the pocket-book, and deposited it in the writing-desk, in which he found, as he had been led to expect, a deed conveying the house to him. He then opened the note lying upon the table, and found its contents accorded with what had just been told him. Placing it with the pocket-book, he locked the writing-desk, exclaiming, "It is useless to struggle further–I must yield to fate!"

This done, he went into the adjoining room, and, casting his eyes about, remarked the antique bottle and flagon. The latter was filled to the brim–how or with what, Auriol paused not to examine; but seizing the cup with desperation, he placed it to his lips, and emptied it at a draught. A species of intoxication, but pleasing as that produced by opium, presently succeeded. All his fears left him, and in their place the gentlest and most delicious fancies arose. Surrendering himself delightedly to their influence, he sank upon a couch, and for some time was wrapped in a dreamy elysium, imagining himself wandering with Edith Talbot in a lovely garden, redolent of sweets, and vocal with the melody of birds. Their path led through a grove, in the midst of which was a fountain; and they were hastening towards its marble brink, when all at once Edith uttered a scream, and, starting back, pointed to a large black snake lying before her, and upon which she would have trodden the next moment. Auriol sprang forward and tried to crush the reptile with his heel; but, avoiding the blow, it coiled around his leg, and plunged its venom teeth into his flesh. The anguish occasioned by the imaginary wound roused him from his slumber, and looking up, he perceived that a servant was in attendance.

Bowing obsequiously, the man inquired whether he had occasion for anything.

"Show me to my bedroom–that is all I require," replied Auriol, scarcely able to shake off the effect of the vision.

And, getting up, he followed the man, almost mechanically, out of the room.

IV. Edith Talbot

It was late when Auriol arose on the following morning. At first, finding himself in a large and most luxuriantly furnished chamber, he was at a loss to conceive how he came there, and it was some time before he could fully recall the mysterious events of the previous night. As had been foretold, however, by Rougemont, his position did not cause him so much anxiety as before.

After attiring himself, he descended to the lower apartments, in one of which a sumptuous breakfast awaited him; and having partaken of it, he took a complete survey of the house, and found it larger and more magnificent even than he had supposed it. He next supplied himself from the pocket-book with a certain sum, for which he fancied he might have occasion in the course of the day, and sallied forth. His first business was to procure a splendid carriage and horse, and to order some new and rich habiliments to be made with the utmost expedition.

He then proceeded towards May Fair, and knocked at the door of a large house at the upper end of Curzon-street. His heart beat violently as he was shown into an elegant drawing-room, and his trepidation momentarily increased, until the servant reappeared and expressed his regret that he had misinformed him in stating that Miss Talbot was at home. Both she and Mr. Talbot, he said, had gone out about half an hour ago. Auriol looked incredulous, but, without making any remark, departed. Hurrying home, he wrote a few lines to Mr. Talbot, announcing the sudden and extraordinary change in his fortune, and formally demanding the hand of Edith. He was about to despatch this letter, when a note was brought him by his servant. It was from Edith. Having ascertained his new address from his card, she wrote to assure him of her constant attachment. Transported by this proof of her affection, Auriol half devoured the note with kisses, and instantly sent off his own letter to her father–merely adding a few words to say that he would call for an answer on the morrow. But he had not to wait thus long for a reply. Ere an hour had elapsed, Mr. Talbot brought it in person.

Mr. Talbot was a man of about sixty–tall, thin, and gentlemanlike in deportment, with grey hair, and black eyebrows, which lent considerable expression to the orbs beneath them. His complexion was a bilious brown, and he possessed none of the good looks which in his daughter had so captivated Auriol, and which it is to be presumed, therefore, she inherited from her mother.

A thorough man of the world, though not an unamiable person, Mr. Talbot was entirely influenced by selfish considerations. He had hitherto looked with an unfavourable eye upon Auriol's attentions to his daughter, from a notion that the connection would be very undesirable in a pecuniary point of view; but the magnificence of the house in Saint James's square, which fully bore out Auriol's account of his newly acquired wealth, wrought a complete change in his opinions, and he soon gave the young man to understand that he should be delighted to have him for a son-in-law. Finding him so favourably disposed, Auriol entreated him to let the marriage take place–within three days, if possible.

Mr. Talbot was greatly grieved that he could not comply with his young friend's request but he was obliged to start the next morning for Nottingham and could not possibly return under three days.

"But we can be married before you go?" cried Auriol.

"Scarcely, I fear," replied Mr. Talbot, smiling blandly. "You must control your impatience, my dear young friend. On the sixth day from this–that is; on Wednesday in next week–we are now at Friday–you shall be made happy."

The coincidence between this appointment and the time fixed by Rougemont for the delivery of his victim, struck Auriol forcibly. His emotion however, escaped Mr. Talbot, who soon after departed, having engaged his future son-in-law to dine with him at seven o'clock.

Auriol it need scarcely be said, was punctual to the hour, or, rather, he anticipated it. He found Edith alone in the drawing-room, and seated near the window, which was filled with choicest flowers. On seeing him, she uttered an exclamation of joy, and sprang to meet him. The young man pressed his lips fervently to the little hand extended to him.

Edith Talbot was a lovely brunette. Her features were regular, and her eyes which were perfectly splendid were dark, almond-shaped, and of almost Oriental languor. Her hair which she wore braided over her brow and gathered behind in a massive roll, was black and glossy as a raven's wing. Her cheeks were dimpled, her lips of velvet softness and her teeth like ranges of pearls. Perfect grace accompanied all her movements, and one only wondered that feet so small as those she possessed should have the power of sustaining a form which, though lightsome, was yet rounded in its proportions.

"You have heard, dear Edith, that your father has consented to our union?" said Auriol, after gazing at her for a few moments in silent admiration.

Edith murmured an affirmative, and blushed deeply.

"He has fixed Wednesday next," pursued Auriol; "but I wish an earlier day could have been named. I have a presentiment that if our marriage is so long delayed, it will not take place at all."

"You are full of misgivings, Auriol," she replied.

"I confess it," he said; "and my apprehensions have risen to such a point that I feel disposed to urge you to a private marriage, during your father's absence."

"Oh, no, Auriol; much as I love you, I could never consent to such a step," she cried. "You cannot urge me to it. I would not abuse my dear father's trusting love. I have never deceived him, and that is the best assurance I can give you that I shall never deceive you."

Further conversation was interrupted by the entrance of Mr. Talbot, who held out both his hands to Auriol, and professed the greatest delight to see him. And no doubt he was sincere. The dinner passed off most pleasantly, and so did the evening; for the old gentleman was in high sprits, and his hilarity was communicated to the young couple. When Auriol and Mr. Talbot went upstairs to tea, they found that Edith's aunt, Mrs. Maitland, had arrived to take charge of her during her father's absence. This lady had always exhibited a partiality for Auriol, and had encouraged his suit to her niece; consequently she was well satisfied with the turn affairs had taken. It was near midnight before Auriol could tear himself away; and when he rose to depart, Mr. Talbot, who had yawned frequently, but fruitlessly, to give him a hint, told him he might depend upon seeing him back on the evening of the third day, and in the meantime he committed him to the care of Mrs. Maitland and Edith.

Three days flew by rapidly and delightfully; and on the evening of the last, just as the little party were assembled in the drawing-room, after dinner, Mr. Talbot returned from his journey. "Well, here I am!" he cried, clasping Edith to his bosom, "without having encountered any misadventure. On the contrary, I have completed my business to my entire satisfaction."

"Oh, how delighted I am to see you dear papa!" exclaimed Edith. "Now, Auriol, you can have no more apprehensions!"

"Apprehensions of what?" cried Mr. Talbot.

"Of some accident befalling you, which might have interfered with our happiness, sir," replied Auriol.

"Oh, lovers are full of idle fears!" cried Mr. Talbot. "They are unreasonable beings. However, here I am, as I said before, safe and sound. Tomorrow we will finish all preliminary arrangements, and the day after you shall be made happy–ha! ha!"

"Do you know, papa, Auriol intends to give a grand ball on our wedding-day, and has invited all his acquaintance to it?" remarked Edith.

"I hope you have not invited Cyprian Rougemont?" said Mr. Talbot, regarding him fixedly. "I have not, sir," replied Auriol turning pale. "But why do you particularize him?"

"Because I have heard some things of him not much to his credit," replied Mr. Talbot. "What–what have you heard, sir?" demanded Auriol.

"Why, one shouldn't believe all the ill one hears of a man; and, indeed, I cannot believe all I have heard of Cyprian Rougemont," replied Mr. Talbot; "but I should be glad if you dropped his acquaintance altogether. And now let us change the subject."

Mr. Talbot seated himself besides Mrs. Maitland, and began to give her some account of his journey, which appeared to have been as pleasant as it had been rapid.

Unable to shake off the gloom which had stolen over him, Auriol took his leave, promising to meet Mr. Talbot at his lawyer's in Lincoln's Inn, at noon on the following day. He was there at the time appointed and, to Mr. Talbot's great delight, and the no small surprise of the lawyer, paid over a hundred thousand pounds, to be settled on his future wife.

"You are a perfect man of honour, Auriol," said Mr. Talbot, clapping him on the shoulder, "and I hope Edith will make you an excellent wife. Indeed, I have no doubt of it."

"Nor I,–if I ever possess her," mentally ejaculated Auriol.

The morning passed in other preparations. In the evening the lovers met as usual, and separated with the full persuasion, on Edith's part at least, that the next day would make them happy. Since the night of the compact, Auriol had neither seen Rougemont, nor heard from him, and he neglected no precaution to prevent his intrusion.

V. The Seventh Night

It was a delicious morning, in May, and the sun shone brightly on Auriol's gorgeous equipage, as he drove to St. George's, Hanover-square, where he was united to Edith. Thus far all seemed auspicious, and he thought he could now bid defiance to fate. With the object of his love close beside him, and linked to him by the strongest and holiest ties, it seemed impossible she could be snatched from him. Nothing occurred during the morning to give him uneasiness, and he gave orders that a carriage and four should be ready an hour before midnight, to convey him and his bride to Richmond, where they were to spend their honeymoon.

Night came, and with it began to arrive the guests who were bidden to the ball. No expense had been spared by Auriol to give splendour to his fete. It was in all respects magnificent. The amusements of the evening commenced with a concert, which was performed by the first singers from the Italian Opera; after which, the ball was opened by Auriol and his lovely bride. As soon as the dance was over, Auriol made a sign to an attendant who instantly disappeared.

"Are you prepared to quit this gay scene with me, Edith?" he asked, with a heart swelling with rapture.

"Quite so," she replied, gazing at him with tenderness; "I long to be alone with you."

"Come then," said Auriol.

Edith arose, and passing her arm under that of her husband, they quitted the ball-room, but in place of descending the principal staircase, they took a more private course. The hall, which they were obliged to cross and which they entered from a side-door, was spacious and beautifully proportioned, and adorned with numerous statues on pedestals. The ceiling was decorated with fresco paintings, and supported by two stately scagliola pillars. From between these, a broad staircase of white marble ascended to the upper room. As Auriol had foreseen, the staircase was thronged with guests ascending to the ballroom, the doors of which being open, afforded glimpses of the dancers, and gave forth strains of liveliest music. Anxious to avoid a newly arrived party in the hall, Auriol and his bride lingered for a moment near a pillar.

"Ha! who is this?" cried Edith, as a tall man, with a sinister countenance, and habited entirely in black moved from the farther side of the pillar, and planted himself in their path, with his back partly towards them.

A thrill of apprehension passed through Auriol's frame. He looked up and beheld Rougemont, who, glancing over his shoulder fixed his malignant gaze upon him. Retreat was now impossible.

"You thought to delude me," said Rougemont, in a deep whisper, audible only to Auriol; "but you counted without your host. I am come to claim my victim."

"What is the matter with you, that you tremble so, dear Auriol?" cried Edith. "Who is this strange person?"

But her husband returned no answer. Terror had taken away his power of utterance.

"Your carriage waits for you at the door, madam–all is pre-pared," said Rougemont, advancing towards her, and taking her hand.

"You are coming, Auriol?" cried Edith, who scarcely knew whether to draw back or go forward.

"Yes–yes," cried Auriol, who fancied he saw a means of escape. "This is my friend, Mr. Rougemont–go with him."

"Mr. Rougemont," cried Edith. "You told my father he would not be here."

"Your husband did not invite me, madam," said Rougemont, with sarcastic emphasis; "but knowing I should be welcome, I came unasked. But let us avoid those persons."

In another moment they were at the door. The carriage was there with its four horses, and a man-servant, in travelling attire, stood be-side the steps. Reassured by the sight, Auriol recovered his courage, and suffered Rougemont to throw a cloak over Edith's shoulders. The next moment she tripped up the steps of the carriage, and was en-sconced within it. Auriol was about to follow her, when he received a violent blow on the chest, which stretched him on the pavement. Be-fore he could regain his feet, Rougemont had sprung into the carriage. The steps were instantly put up by the man-servant, who mounted the box with the utmost celerity, while the postilions, plunging spurs into their horses, dashed off with lightning speed. As the carriage turned the corner of King-street, Auriol, who had just arisen, beheld, by the light of a lamp, Rougemont's face at the window of the carriage, charged with an expression of the most fiendish triumph.

"What is the matter?" cried Mr. Talbot, who had approached Auriol. "I came to bid you good-bye. Why do I find you here alone? Where is the carriage?–what has become of Edith?"

"She is in the power of the Fiend, and I have sold her to him," replied Auriol, gloomily.

"What mean you, wretch?" cried Mr. Talbot, in a voice of distraction. "I heard that Cyprian Rougemont was here. Can it be he that has gone off with her?"

"You have hit the truth," replied Auriol. "He bought her with the money I gave you. I have sold her and myself to perdition!"

"Horror!" exclaimed the old man, falling backwards.

"Ay, breathe your last–breathe your last!" cried Auriol, wildly. "Would I could yield up my life, likewise!"

And he hurried away, utterly unconscious whither he went.

Book the Second – Cyprian de Rougemont

I. The cell

Mr. Thorneycroft and his companions had scarcely gained a passage in the deserted house, which they had entered in the manner described in a previous chapter, when they were alarmed by the sudden and furious ringing of a bell overhead. The noise brought them instantly to a halt, and each man grasped his arms in expectation of an attack, but the peal ceasing in a few moments, and all continuing quiet, they moved on as before, and presently reached a large hall with a lofty window over the door, which, being without shutters, afforded light enough to reveal the dilapidated condition of the mansion.

From this hall four side doors opened, apparently communicating with different chambers, three of which were cautiously tried by Reeks, but they proved to be fastened. The fourth, however, yielded to his touch, and admitted them to a chamber, which seemed to have been recently occupied, for a lamp was burning within it. The walls were panelled with dusty oak, and hung at the lower end with tapestry, representing the Assyrian monarch Ninus, and his captive Zoroaster, King of the Bactrians. The chief furniture consisted of three large high-backed and grotesquely carved arm-chairs, near one of which stood a powerful electrical machine. Squares and circles were traced upon the floor, and here and there were scattered cups and balls, and other matters apparently belonging to a conjuring apparatus.

The room might be the retreat of a man of science, or it might be the repository of a juggler. But whoever its occupant was, and whatsoever his pursuits, the good things of the world were not altogether neglected by him, as was proved by a table spread with viands, and furnished with glasses, together with a couple of taper-necked bottles.

While glancing upwards, Mr. Thorneycroft remarked that just above each chair the ceiling was pierced with a round hole, the meaning of which he could not at the time comprehend, though after circumstances sufficiently explained it to him.

"A singular room," he observed to Reeks, on concluding his survey. "Did you expect to find anyone here?"

"I hardly know," replied the other. "That bell may have given the alarm. But I will soon ascertain the point. Remain here till I return."

"You are not going to leave us?" rejoined Mr. Thorneycroft, uneasily.

"Only for a moment," said Reeks. "Keep quiet, and no harm will befall you. Whatever you may hear without, do not stir."

"What are we likely to hear?" asked Thorneycroft, with increasing trepidation.

"That's impossible to say," answered Reeks; "but I warn you not to cry out unnecessarily, as such an imprudence would endanger our safety."

"You are quite sure you don't mean to abandon us?" persisted Thorneycroft.

"Make yourself easy; I have no such intention," rejoined Reeks, sternly.

"Oh! ve'll take care of you, don't be afeerd, old gent," said Ginger.

"Yes, ve'll take care on you," added the Tinker and the Sandman.

"You may depend upon them as upon me, sir," said Reeks. "Before we explore the subterranean apartments, I wish to see whether anyone is upstairs."

"Wot's that you say about subterranean apartments, Mr. Reeks?" interposed Ginger. "Ye ain't a-goin' below, eh?"

But without paying any attention to the inquiry, Reeks quitted the room, and closed the door carefully after him. He next crossed the hall, and cautiously ascending a staircase at the farther end of it, reached the landing-place. Beyond it was a gallery, from which several chambers opened.

Advancing a few paces, he listened intently, and hearing a slight sound in an apartment to the right, he stepped softly towards it, and placing his eye to the keyhole, beheld a tall man, dressed in black pacing to and fro with rapid strides, while three other persons, wrapped in sable gowns, and disguised with hideous masks, stood silent and motionless at a little distance from him. In the tall man he recognised Cyprian Rougemont. Upon a table in the middle of the room was laid a large open volume, bound in black vellum. Near it stood a lamp, which served to illumine the scene.

Suddenly, Rougemont stopped, and turning over several leaves of the book, which were covered with cabalistic characters, appeared in search of some magic formula. Before he could find it, however, a startling interruption occurred. An alarum-bell, fixed against the wall, began to ring, and at the same moment the doors of a cabinet flew open, and a large ape (for such it seemed to Reeks), clothed in a woollen shirt and drawers, sprang forth, and bounding upon the table beside Rougemont, placed its mouth to his ear. The communication thus strangely made seemed highly displeasing to Rougemont, who knitted his brows, and delivered some instructions in an under tone to the monkey. The animal nodded its head in token of obedience, jumped off the table, and bounded back to the cabinet, the doors of which closed as before. Rougemont next took up the lamp, with the evident intention of quitting the room, seeing which, Reeks hastily retreated to an adjoining chamber, the door of which was fortunately open, and had scarcely gained its shelter when the four mysterious personages appeared on the gallery. Reeks heard their footsteps descending the staircase, and then, creeping cautiously after them, watched them across the hall, and pause before the chamber containing Mr. Thorneycroft and his companions. After a moment's deliberation, Rougemont noiselessly locked the door, took out the key, and leaving two of his attendants on guard, returned with the third towards the staircase.

Without tarrying to confront them, Reeks started back, and hurried along the gallery till he came to a back staircase, which conducted him, by various descents, to the basement floor, where, after traversing one or two vaults, he entered a subterranean passage, arched overhead, and having several openings at the sides, apparently communicating with other passages. It was lighted at intervals by lamps, which emitted a feeble radiance.

By the light of one of these, Reeks discovered the door of a cell. It was of iron, and as he struck it with his hand, returned a hollow clangour. On repeating the blow, a hoarse voice from within cried, "Leave me in peace!"

"Is it Auriol Darcy who speaks?" demanded Reeks.

"It is," replied the prisoner. "Who are you that put the question?"

"A friend," replied Reeks.

"I have no friend here," said Auriol.

"You are mistaken," rejoined Reeks. "I have come with Mr. Thorneycroft to deliver you."

"Mr. Thorneycroft has come too late. He has lost his daughter," replied Auriol.

"What has happened to her?" demanded Reeks.

"She is in the power of the Fiend," replied Auriol.

"I know she is detained by Cyprian Rougemont," said Reeks. "But what has befallen her."

"She has become like his other victims–like my victims!" cried Auriol, distractedly.

"Do not despair," rejoined Reeks. "She may yet be saved."

"Saved! how?" cried Auriol. "All is over."

"So it may seem to you," rejoined Reeks; "but you are the victim of delusion."

"Oh! that I could think so!" exclaimed Auriol. "But no–I saw her fall into the pit. I beheld her veiled figure rise from it. I witnessed her signature to the fatal scroll. There could be no illusion in what I then beheld."

"Despite all this, you will see her again," said Reeks.

"Who are you who give me this promise?" asked Auriol.

"As I have already declared, a friend," replied Reeks.

"Are you human?"

"As yourself."

"Then you seek in vain to struggle with the powers of darkness," said Auriol.

"I have no fear of Cyprian Rougemont," rejoined Reeks, with a laugh.

"Your voice seems familiar to me," said Auriol. "Tell me who you are?"

"You shall know anon," replied Reeks. "But, hist!–we are interrupted. Someone approaches."

II. The Enchanted Chairs

More than ten minutes had elapsed since Reek's departure, and Mr. Thorneycroft, who had hitherto had some difficulty in repressing his anger, now began to give vent to it in muttered threats and complaints. His impatience was shared by the Tinker, who, stepping up to

Ginger, said–"Wot the devil can Mr. Reeks be about? I hope nuffin' has happened to him."

"Don't mention a certain gent's name here," remarked Ginger; "or if you do, treat it vith proper respect."

"Pshaw!" exclaimed the Tinker, impatiently; "I don't like a man stayin' avay in this manner. It looks suspicious. I wotes ve goes and sees arter him. Ve can leave the old gent to take a keviet nap by himself. Don't disturb yourself, sir. Ve'll only jist giv' a look about us, and then come back."

"Stay where you are, rascal!" cried Thorneycroft, angrily. "I won't be left. Stay where you are, I command you!"

"Vell, ve've got a noo captain, I'm a-thinkin'," said the Tinker, winking at the others. "Ve've no vish to disobleege you, sir. I'll only jist peep out into the hall, and see if Mr. Reeks is anyvhere thereabouts. Vy, zounds!" he added, as he tried the door, "it's locked!"

"What's locked?" cried Thorneycroft, in dismay.

"The door, to be sure," replied the Tinker. "Ve're prisoners."

"Oh Lord, you don't say so!" cried the iron-merchant, in an agony of fright. "What will become of us?"

A roar of laughter from the others converted his terror into fury

"I see how it is," he cried. "You have entrapped me, ruffians. It's all a trick. You mean to murder me. But I'll sell my life dearly. The first one who approaches shall have his brains blown out." And as he spoke, he levelled a pistol at the Tinker's head.

"Holloa! wot are you arter, sir?" cried the individual, sheltering his head with his hands. "You're a labourin' under a mistake–a complete mistake. If it is a trap, ve're catched in it as vall as yourself."

"To be sure ve is," added the Sandman. "Sit down, and vait a bit. I dessay Mr. Reeks'll come back, and it von't do no good gettin' into a passion."

"Well, well, I must resign myself, I suppose," groaned Thorneycroft, sinking into a chair. "It's a terrible situation to be placed in–shut up in a haunted house."

"I've been in many much vurser sitivations," observed Ginger, "and I alvays found the best vay to get out on 'em wos to take things quietly."

"Besides, there's no help for it," said the Tinker, seating himself.

"That remains to be seen," observed the Sandman, taking the chair opposite Thorneycroft. "If Reeks don't come back soon, I'll bust open the door."

"Plenty o' time for that," said Ginger, sauntering towards the table on which the provisions were spread; "wot do you say to a mouthful o' wittles?"

"I wouldn't touch 'em for the world," replied the Sandman.

"Nor I," added the Tinker; "they may be poisoned."

"Poisoned–nonsense!" cried Ginger; "don't you see some von has been a-takin' his supper here? I'll jist finish it for him."

"Vith all my 'art," said the Tinker.

"Don't touch it on any account," cried Mr. Thorneycroft. "I agree with your companions, it may be poisoned."

"Oh! I ain't afeerd," cried Ginger, helping himself to a dish before him. "As good a pigeon-pie as ever I tasted. Your health, Mr. Thorneycroft," he added, filling a goblet from one of the bottles. "My service to you, gents. Famous tipple, by Jove!" drawing a long breath after the draught, and smacking his lips with amazing satisfaction.

"Never tasted sich a glass o' wine in all my born days," he continued, replenishing the goblet: "I wonder wot it's called?"

"Prussic acid," replied Mr. Thorneycroft, gruffly.

"Proossic fiddlesticks," cried Ginger; "more likely Tokay. I shall finish the bottle, and never be the vorse for it!"

"He's gettin' svipy," said the Tinker. "I vonder vether it's really Tokay?"

"No such thing," cried Thorneycroft; "let him alone."

"I must taste it," said the Tinker, unable to resist the temptation. "Here, give us a glass, Ginger!"

"Vith pleasure," replied Ginger, filling a goblet to the brim, and handing it to him. "You'd better be perwailed upon, Sandy."

"Vell, I s'pose I must," replied the Sandman, taking the goblet proffered him.

"Here's the beak's healths!" cried Ginger. "I gives that toast 'cos they're alvays so kind to us dog-fanciers."

"Dog-fanciers–say, rather, dog-stealers; for that's the name such vagabonds deserve to be known by," said Mr. Thorneycroft, with some asperity.

"Vell, ve von't quarrel about names," replied Ginger, laughing, "but I'll relate a circumstance to you as'll prove that wotever your opinion of our wocation may be, the beaks upholds it."

"There can be but one opinion as to your nefarious profession," said Mr. Thorneycroft, "and that is, that it's as bad as horse-stealing and sheep-stealing, and should be punished as those offences are punished."

"So I think, sir," said Ginger, winking at the others; "but to my story, and don't interrupt me, or I can't get through vith it properly. There's a gent livin' not a hundred miles from Pall-Mall, as the noospapers says, as had a favourite Scotch terrier, not worth more nor half-a-crown to any one but hisself, but highly wallerable to him, 'cos it wos a favourite. Vell, the dog is lost. A pal of mine gets hold on it, and the gent soon offers a reward for its recovery. This don't bring it back quite so soon as he expects, 'cos he don't offer enough; so he goes to an agent, Mr. Simpkins, in the Edger-road, and Mr. Simpkins says to him–says he, 'How are you, sir? I expected you some days ago. You've com'd about that ere Scotch terrier. You've got a wallable greyhound, I understand. A man told me he'd have that afore long.' Seein' the gent stare, Mr. S. adds, 'Vel, I'll tell you wot you must give for your dog. The party von't take less than six guineas. He knows it ain't vorth six shillin', but it's a great favourite, and has given him a precious sight o' trouble in gettin' it.' 'Give him trouble!' cries the gent, angrily–'and what has it given me? I hope to see the rascal hanged! I shall pay no such money.' 'Werry vell,' replies Mr. Simpkins, coolly, 'then your dog'll be bled to death, as the nobleman's wos, and thrown down a breathless carkis afore your door.'

"You don't mean to say that such a horrid circumstance as that really took place?" cried Thorneycroft, who was much interested in the relation.

"Only t'other day, I assure you," replied Ginger.

"I'd shoot the ruffian who treated a dog of mine so, if I caught him!" cried Mr. Thorneycroft, indignantly.

"And sarve him right, too," said Ginger. "I discourages all cruelty to hanimals. But don't interrupt me again. Arter a bit more chafferin' vith Mr. Simphins, the gent offers three pound for his dog, and then goes avay; Next day he reads a report i' the Times noospaper that a man has been taken up for dog-stealin', and that a lot o' dogs is shut up in the green-yard behind the police-office in Bow-street So he goes there in search o' his favourite, and sure enough he finds it, but the inspector von't give it up to him, 'cos the superintendent is out o' the vay."

WILLIAM HARRISON AINSWORTH

"Shameful!" cried Mr. Thorneycroft.

"Shameful, indeed, sir," echoed Ginger, laughing. "Thinkin' his dog safe enough in the hands o' the police, the gent sleeps soundly that night, but ven he goes back next mornin' he finds it has disappeared. The green-yard has been broken into overnight, and all the dogs stolen from it."

"Under the noses of the police," cried Thorneycroft.

"Under their werry noses," replied Ginger. "But now comes the cream o' the jest. You shall hear wot the beak says to him ven the gent craves his assistance. 'I can't interfere in the matter,' says he, a-bendin' of his brows in a majestic manner. 'Parties don't ought to come here vith complaints of vhich I can't take notice. This place ain't an adver-tisin' office, and I shan't suffer it to be made von. I von't listen to statements affectin' the characters of absent parties.' Statements af-fectin' our characters,–do you tvig that, sir?"

"I do, indeed," said Thorneycroft, sighing; "and I am sorry to think such a remark should have dropped from the bench."

"You're right to say it dropped from it, sir," laughed Ginger.

"I told you the beaks vos our best friends; they alvays takes our parts. Ven the gent urges that it was a subject of ser'ous importance to dog-owners, the magistrit angrily interrupts him, sayin'–'Then let there be a meetin' of dog-owners to discuss their grievances. Don't come to me. I can't help you.' And he vouldn't if he could, 'cos he's the dog-fancier's friend."

"It looks like it, I must own," replied Thorneycroft. "Such repre-hensible indifference gives encouragement to people of your profession. Government itself is to blame. As all persons who keep dogs pay a tax for them, their property ought to be protected."

"I'm quite satisfied vith the present state of the law," said Gin-ger; "here's the vorthy beak! I'll drink his health for a second time."

99

"Halloa! wot's that?" cried the Tinker; "I thought I heerd a noise."

"So did I," rejoined the Sandman; "a strange sort o' rumblin' sound overhead."

"There it goes again!" cried Ginger; "wot an awful din!"

"Now it's underneath," said Mr. Thorneycroft, turning pale, and trembling. "It sounds as if some hidden machinery were at work."

The noise, which up to this moment had borne an indistinct resemblance to the creaking of wheels and pulleys, now increased to a violent clatter, while the house was shaken as if by the explosion of a mine beneath it.

At the same time, the occupants of the chairs received a sharp electrical shock, that agitated every limb, and caused Mr. Thorneycroft to let fall his pistol, which went off as it reached the ground. At the same time, the Sandman dropped his goblet, and the Tinker relinquished his grasp of the cutlass. Before they could recover from the shock, all three were caught by stout wooden hooks, which, detaching themselves from the back of the chairs, pinioned their arms, while their legs were restrained by fetters, which sprang from the ground and clasped round their ankles. Thus fixed, they struggled vainly to get free. The chairs seemed nailed to the ground, so that all efforts to move them proved futile.

But the worst was to come. From the holes in the ceiling already alluded to, descended three heavy bell-shaped helmets, fashioned like those worn by divers at the bottom of the sea, and having round eyelet-holes of glass. It was evident, from the manner of their descent, that these helmets must drop on the heads of the sitters–a conviction that filled them with inexpressible terror. They shouted, and swore frightfully; but their vociferations availed them nothing. Down came the helmets, and the same moment the monkey which had been seen by Reeks issued from a cupboard at the top of a cabinet, and grinned and gibbered at them.

Down came the first helmet, and covered the Tinker to the shoulders. His appearance was at once ludicrous and terrible, and his roaring within the casque sounded like the bellowing of a baited bull.

Down came the second helmet, though rather more slowly, and the Sandman was eclipsed in the same manner as the Tinker, and roared as loudly.

In both these instances the helmets had dropped without guidance, but in the case of Mr. Thorneycroft, a hand, thrust out of the hole in the ceiling, held the helmet suspended over his head, like the sword of Damocles. While the poor iron-merchant momentarily expected the same doom as his companions, his attention was attracted towards the monkey, which, clinging with one hand to the side of the cabinet, extended the other skinny arm towards him, and exclaimed–"Will you swear to go hence if you are spared?"

"No, I will not," replied the iron-merchant. He had scarcely spoken, when the helmet fell with a jerk, and extinguished him like the others.

Ginger alone remained. During the whole of this strange scene, he had stood with the bottle in hand, transfixed with terror and astonishment, and wholly unable to move or cry out. A climax was put to his fright, by the descent of the three chairs, with their occupants, through the floor into a vault beneath; and as the helmets were whisked up again to the ceiling, and the trap-doors closed upon the chairs, he dropped the bottle, and fell with his face upon the table. He was, however, soon roused by a pull at his hair, while a shrill voice called him by his name.

"Who is it?" groaned the dog-fancier.

"Look up!" cried the speaker, again plucking his hair.

Ginger complied, and beheld the monkey seated beside him. "Vy, it can't be, surely," he cried. "And yet I could almost svear it was Old Parr."

"You're near the mark," replied the other, with a shrill laugh. "It is your venerable friend."

"Vot the deuce are you doing here, and in this dress, or rayther undress?" inquired Ginger. "Ven I see you this mornin', you wos in the service of Mr. Loftus."

"I've got a new master since then," replied the dwarf.

"I'm sorry to hear it," said Ginger, shaking his head. "You hav'n't sold yourself, like Doctor Forster—"

"Faustus, my dear Ginger–not Forster," corrected Old Parr. "No, no, I've made a bargain. And to be plain with you, I've no desire to remain long in my present master's service."

"I don't like to ask the question too directly, wenerable," said Ginger, in a deprecatory tone–"but is your master–hem!–is he–hem!–the–the–"

"The devil, you would say," supplied Old Parr. "Between ourselves, I'm afraid there's no denying it."

"La! wot a horrible idea!" exclaimed Ginger with a shudder; "it makes the flesh creep on one's bones. Then we're in your master's power?"

"Very like it," replied Old Parr.

"And there ain't no chance o' deliverance?"

"None that occurs to me."

"Oh Lord! oh Lord!" groaned Ginger; "I'll repent. I'll become a reformed character. I'll never steal dogs no more."

"In that case, there may be some chance for you," said Old Parr. "I think I could help you to escape. Come with me, and I'll try and get you out."

"But wot is to become of the others?" demanded Ginger.

"Oh, leave them to their fate," replied Old Parr.

"No, that'll never do," cried Ginger. "Ve're all in the same boat, and must row out together the best vay ve can. I tell you wot it is, wenerable," he added, seizing him by the throat–"your master may be the devil, but you're mortal; and if you don't help me to deliver my companions, I'll squeeze your windpipe for you."

"That's not the way to induce me to help you," said Old Parr, twisting himself like an eel out of the other's grip. "Now get out, if you can."

"Don't be angry," cried Ginger, seeing the mistake he had committed, and trying to conciliate him; "I only meant to frighten you a bit. Can you tell me if Mr. Auriol Darcy is here?"

"Yes, he is, and a close prisoner," replied Old Parr.

"And the girl–Miss Ebber, wot of her?"

"I can't say," rejoined Old Parr. "I can only speak to the living."

"Then she's dead!" cried Ginger, with a look of horror.

"That's a secret," replied the dwarf, mysteriously; "and I'm bound by a terrible oath not to disclose it."

"I'll have it out of you notvithstandin'," muttered Ginger. "I vish you would lend me a knock on the head, old feller. I can't help thinkin' I've got a terrible fit o' the nightmare."

"Let this waken you, then," said Old Parr, giving him a sound buffet on the ear.

"Holloa, wenerable! not so hard!" cried Ginger.

"Ha! ha! ha!" screamed the dwarf. "You know what you're about now."

"Not exactly," said Ginger. "I vish I wos fairly out o' this cursed place!"

"You shouldn't have ventured into the lion's den," said Old Parr, in a taunting tone. "But come with me, and perhaps I may be able to do something towards your liberation."

So saying, he drew aside the tapestry, and opened a panel behind it, through which he passed, and beckoned Ginger to follow him. Taking a pistol from his pocket, the latter complied.

III. Gerrard Paston

Before the chair, in which Mr. Thorneycroft was fixed, reached the ground terror had taken away his senses. A bottle of salts, placed to his nose, revived him after a time; but he had nearly relapsed into insensibility on seeing two strange figures, in hideous masks and sable cloaks, standing on either side of him, while at a little distance was a third, who carried a strangely fashioned lantern. He looked round for his companions in misfortune, but, though the chairs were there, they were unoccupied.

The masked attendants paid no attention to the iron-merchant's cries and entreaties; but as soon as they thought him able to move, they touched a spring, which freed his arms and legs from their bondage, and raising him, dragged him out of the vault, and along a narrow passage, till they came to a large sepulchral-looking chamber, cased with black marble, in the midst of which, on a velvet fauteuil of the same hue as the walls, sat Cyprian Rougemont. It was, in fact, the chamber where Ebba had been subject to her terrible trial.

Bewildered with terror, the poor iron-merchant threw himself at the feet of Rougemont, who, eyeing him with a look of malignant triumph, cried.

"You have come to seek your daughter. Behold her!"

And at the words, the large black curtains at the farther end of the room were suddenly withdrawn, and discovered the figure of Ebba Thorneycroft standing at the foot of the marble staircase. Her features were as pale as death; her limbs rigid and motionless; but her eyes blazed with preternatural light. On beholding her, Mr. Thorneycroft uttered a loud cry, and, springing to his feet would have rushed towards her, but he was held back by the two masked attendants, who seized each arm, and detained him by main force.

"Ebba?" he cried–"Ebba!"

But she appeared wholly insensible to his cries, and remained in the same attitude, with her eyes turned away from him.

"What ails her?" cried the agonized father. "Ebba! Ebba!"

"Call louder," said Rougemont, with a jeering laugh.

"Do you not know me? do you not hear me?" shrieked Mr. Thorneycroft.

Still the figure remained immovable.

"I told you you should see her," replied Rougemont, in a taunting tone; "but she is beyond your reach."

"Not so, not so!" cried Thorneycroft. "Come to me, Ebba!–come to your father. Oh, Heaven! she hears me not! she heeds me not! Her senses are gone."

"She is fast bound by a spell," said Rougemont. "Take a last look at her. You will see her no more."

And, stretching out his hand, the curtains slowly descended, and shrouded the figure from view.

Thorneycroft groaned aloud.

"Are you not content?" cried Rougemont. "Will you depart in peace, and swear never to come here more? If so, I will liberate you and your companions."

"So far from complying with your request, I swear never to rest till I have rescued my child from you, accursed being!" cried Thorneycroft energetically.

"You have sealed your doom, then," replied Rougemont. "But before you are yourself immured, you shall see how Auriol Darcy is circumstanced. Bring him along."

And, followed by the attendants, who dragged Mr. Thorneycroft after him, he plunged into an opening on the right. A few steps brought him to the entrance of the cell. Touching the heavy iron door, it instantly swung open, and disclosed Auriol chained to a stone at the farther corner of the narrow chamber.

Not a word was spoken for some minutes, but the captives regarded each other piteously. "Oh, Mr. Thorneycroft," cried Auriol, at length, "I beseech you forgive me. I have destroyed your daughter."

"You!" exclaimed the iron-merchant, in astonishment.

"It is true," said Rougemont.

"I would have saved her if it had been possible!" cried Auriol. "I warned her that to love me would be fatal to her. I told her I was linked to an inexorable destiny, which would involve her in its meshes–but in vain."

"Oh!" ejaculated Thorneycroft.

"You see you ought to blame him, not me," said Rougemont, with a derisive laugh.

"I would have given my life, my soul, to preserve her, had it been possible!" cried Auriol.

"Horrors crowd so thick upon me that my brain reels," cried Thorneycroft "Merciless wretch!" he added, to Rougemont, "fiend—whatever you are, complete your work of ruin by my destruction. I have nothing left to tie me to life."

"I would have the miserable live," said Rougemont, with a diabolical laugh. "It is only the happy I seek to destroy. But you have to thank your own obstinacy for your present distress. Bid a lasting farewell to Auriol. You will see him no more."

"Hold!" exclaimed Auriol. "A word before we part."

"Ay, hold!" echoed a loud and imperious voice, from the depths of the passage.

"Ha!—who speaks?" demanded Rougemont, a shade passing over his countenance.

"I, Gerard Paston!" exclaimed Reeks, stepping forward. The crape was gone from his brow, and in its place was seen the handsome and resolute features of a man of middle life. He held a pistol in either hand.

"Is it you, Gerard Paston?" cried Auriol, regarding him; "the brother of Clara, my second victim!"

"It is," replied the other. "Your deliverance is at hand, Auriol."

"And you have dared to penetrate here, Gerard?" cried Rougemont, stamping the ground with rage. "Recollect, you are bound to me by the same ties as Auriol, and you shall share his fate."

"I am not intimidated by threats," replied Paston, with a scornful laugh. "You have employed your arts too long. Deliver up Auriol and this gentleman at once, or—" And he levelled the pistols at him.

"Fire!" cried Rougemont, drawing himself up to his towering height. "No earthly bullets can injure me."

"Ve'll try that!" cried Ginger, coming up at the moment behind Paston.

And he discharged a pistol, with a deliberate aim, at the breast of Rougemont. The latter remained erect, and apparently uninjured.

"You see how ineffectual your weapons are," said Rougemont, with a derisive laugh.

"It must be the devil!" cried Ginger running off.

"I will try mine," said Paston.

But before he could draw the triggers, the pistols were wrested from his grasp by the two attendants, who had quitted Thorneycroft, and stolen upon him unperceived, and who next pinioned his arms.

IV. The Pit

So bewildered was the poor iron-merchant by the strange and terrible events that had befallen him, that, though released by the two masked attendants, who left him, as before related, to seize Gerard Paston, he felt utterly incapable of exertion, and would probably have made no effort to regain his freedom, if his coat had not been vigorously plucked behind, while a low voice urged him to fly. Glancing in the direction of the friendly speaker, he could just discern a diminutive object standing within the entrance of a side-passage, and reared up against the wall so as to be out of sight of Rougemont and his attendants. It was the monkey—or rather Old Parr—who, continuing to tug violently at his coat, at last succeeded in drawing him backwards into the passage, and then grasping his hand tightly, hurried him along it. The passage was wholly unlighted, but Mr. Thorneycroft could perceive that it was exceedingly circuitous, and winded round like a maze.

"Where are you taking me?" he inquired, attempting to stop.

"Ask no questions," rejoined the dwarf, pulling him along. "Do you want to be captured, and shut up in a cell for the rest of your life?"

"Certainly not," replied Thorneycroft, accelerating his movements; "I hope there's no chance of it."

"There's every chance of it," rejoined Old Parr. "If you're taken, you'll share Auriol's fate."

"Oh, Lord! I hope not," groaned the iron-merchant. "I declare, you frighten me so much that you take away all power of movement. I shall drop in a minute."

"Come along, I say," screamed the dwarf. "I hear them close behind us."

And as he spoke, shouts, and the noise of rapidly approaching footsteps, resounded along the passage.

"I can't stir another step," gasped the iron-merchant. "I'm completely done. Better yield at once."

"What, without a struggle?" cried the dwarf, tauntingly. "Think of your daughter, and let the thought of her nerve your heart. She is lost for ever, if you don't get out of this accursed place."

"She is lost for ever as it is," cried the iron-merchant despairingly.

"No—she may yet be saved," rejoined the dwarf. "Come on—come one—they are close behind us."

And it was evident, from the increased clamour, that their pursuers were upon them.

Roused by the imminence of the danger, and by the hope of rescuing his daughter, Mr. Thorneycroft exerted all his energies, and sprang forward. A little farther on, they were stopped by a door. It was closed; and venting his disappointment in a scream, the dwarf searched for the handle, but could not find it.

"We are entrapped—we shall be caught," he cried, "and then woe to both of us. Fool that I was to attempt your preservation. Better I had left you to rot in a dungeon than have incurred Rougemont's displeasure."

The iron-merchant replied by a groan.

"It's all over with me," he said. "I give it up—I'll die here!"

"No—we are saved," cried the dwarf, as the light, now flashing strongly upon the door, revealed a small iron button within it,—"saved—saved!"

As he spoke, he pressed against the button, which moved a spring, and the door flew open. Just as they passed through it, the two masked attendants came in sight. The dwarf instantly shut the door, and finding a bolt on the side next him, shot it into the socket. Scarcely had he accomplished this, when the pursuers came up, and dashed themselves against the door; but finding it bolted, presently ceased their efforts, and apparently withdrew.

"They are gone by some other way to intercept us," cried Old Parr, who had paused for a moment to listen; "come on, Mr. Thorney-croft."

"I'll try," replied the iron-merchant, with a subdued groan, "but I'm completely spent. Oh, that I ever ventured into this place!"

"It's too late to think of that now; besides, you came here to rescue your daughter," rejoined Old Parr. "Take care and keep near me. I wonder where this passage leads to?"

"Don't you know?" inquired the iron-merchant.

"Not in the least," returned the dwarf. "This is the first time I've been here–and it shall be the last, if I'm allowed any choice in the matter."

"You haven't told me how you came here at all," observed Thorneycroft.

"I hardly know myself," replied the dwarf; "but I find it more difficult to get out than I did to get in. How this passage twists about. I declare we seem to be returning to the point we started from."

"I think we are turning round ourselves," cried Thorneycroft, in an agony of fright. "My head is going. Oh dear! oh dear!"

"Why it does seem very strange, I must say," remarked the dwarf, coming to a halt. "I could almost fancy that the solid stone walls were moving around us."

"They are moving," cried Thorneycroft, stretching out his hand. "I feel 'em. Lord have mercy upon us, and deliver us from the power of the Evil One!"

"The place seems on fire," cried the dwarf. "A thick smoke fills the passage. Don't you perceive it, Mr. Thorneycroft?"

"Don't I!–to be sure I do," cried the iron-merchant, coughing and sneezing. "I feel as if I were in a room with a smoky chimney, and no window open. Oh!–oh!–I'm choking!"

"Don't mind it," cried the dwarf, who seemed quite at his ease. "We shall soon be out of the smoke."

"I can't stand it," cried Mr. Thorneycroft; "I shall die. Oh! poah–pish–puff!"

"Come on, I tell you–you'll get some fresh air in a minute," rejoined Old Parr. "Halloa! how's this? No outlet. We're come to a dead stop."

111

"Dead stop, indeed!" echoed the iron-merchant. "We've come to that long ago. But what new difficulty has arisen?"

"Merely that the road's blocked up by a solid wall–that's all," replied Old Parr.

"Blocked up!" exclaimed Thorneycroft. "Then we're entombed alive."

"I am," said the dwarf, with affected nonchalance. "As to you, you've the comfort of knowing it'll soon be over with you. But for me, nothing can harm me."

"Don't be too sure of that," cried a voice above them.

"Did you speak, Mr. Thorneycroft?" asked the dwarf.

"N-o-o–not I," gasped the iron-merchant. "I'm suffocating–help to drag me out."

"Get out if you can," cried the voice that had just spoken.

"It's Rougemont himself," cried the dwarf, in alarm. "Then there's no escape."

"None whatever, rascal," replied the unseen speaker. "I want you. I have more work for you to do."

"I won't leave Mr. Thorneycroft," cried the dwarf, resolutely. "I've promised to preserve him, and I'll keep my word."

"Fool!" cried the other. "You must obey when I command."

And as the words were uttered, a hand was thrust down from above, which, grasping the dwarf by the nape of the neck, drew him upwards.

"Lay hold of me, Mr. Thorneycroft," screamed Old Parr. "I'm going up again–lay hold of me–pull me down."

Well-nigh stifled by the thickening and pungent vapour, the poor iron-merchant found compliance impossible. Before he could reach the dwarf, the little fellow was carried off. Left to himself, Mr. Thorney-croft staggered along the passage, expecting every moment to drop, until at length a current of fresh air blew in his face, and enabled him to breathe more freely. Some what revived, he went on, but with great deliberation, and it was well he did so, for he suddenly arrived at the brink of a pit about eight feet in depth, into which, if he had ap-proached it incautiously, he must infallibly have stumbled, and in all probability have broken his neck. This pit evidently communicated with a lower range of chambers, as was shown by a brazen lamp burn-ing under an archway. A ladder was planted at one side, and by this Mr. Thorneycroft descended, but scarcely had he set foot on the ground, than he felt himself rudely grasped by a man who stepped from under the archway. The next moment, however, he was released, while the familiar voice of the Tinker exclaimed.

"Vy, bless my 'art, if it ain't Mister Thorneycroft."

"Yes, it's me, certainly, Mr. Tinker," replied the iron-merchant. "Who's that you've got with you?"

"Vy, who should it be but the Sandman," rejoined the other, gruffly. "Ve've set ourselves free at last, and have made some nice diskiveries into the bargin."

"Yes, ve've found it all out, added the Tinker.

"What have you discovered–what have you found out?" cried the iron-merchant, breathlessly. "Have you found my daughter? Where is she? Take me to her."

"Not so fast, old gent, not so fast," rejoined the Tinker. "Ye ain't sure as 'ow ve've found your darter, but ve've catched a peep of a nice young 'ooman."

"Oh! it must be her no doubt of it," cried the iron-merchant. "Where is she? Take me to her without a moment's delay."

"But ve can't get to her, I tell 'ee," replied the Tinker, "Ye knows the place 'vere she's a-shut up,–that's all."

"Take me to it," cried Mr. Thorneycroft, eagerly.

"Yell, if you must go, step this vay, then," rejoined the Tinker, proceeding towards the archway. "Halloa, Sandy, did you shut the door arter you?"

"Not I," replied the other; "open it."

"Easily said," rejoined the Tinker, "but not quevite so easily done. Vy, zounds, it's shut of itself and bolted itself on t'other side!"

"Someone must have followed you," groaned Thorneycroft. "We're watched on all sides."

"Ay, and from above, too," cried the Sandman. "Look up there!" he added, in accents of alarm.

"What's the matter? What new danger is at hand?" inquired the iron-merchant.

"Look up, I say," cried the Sandman. "Don't ye see, Tinker?"

"Ay, ay, I see," replied the other. "The roof's a-comin' in upon us. Let's get out o' this as fast as ve can." And he kicked and pushed against the door, but all his efforts were unavailing to burst it open.

At the same time the Sandman rushed towards the ladder, but before he could mount it all egress by that means was cut off. An immense iron cover worked in a groove was pushed by some unseen machinery over the top of the pit, and enclosed them in it.

V. New Perplexities

For several hours deep sleep, occasioned by some potent medicaments, had bound up the senses of Auriol. On awaking, he found himself within a cell, the walls, the floor, and the ceiling of which were of solid stone masonry. In the midst of this chamber, and supporting the ponderous roof, stood a massive granite pillar, the capital of which was grotesquely ornamented with death's-heads and crossbones, and against this pillar leaned Auriol, with his left arm chained by heavy links of iron to a ring in the adjoining wall. Beside him stood a pitcher of water, and near him lay an antique-looking book, bound in black vellum. The dungeon in which he was confined was circular in form, with a coved roof, sustained by the pillar before mentioned, and was approached by a steep flight of steps rising from a doorway, placed some six feet below the level of the chamber, and surmounted by a pointed arch. A stream of light, descending from a narrow aperture in the roof, fell upon his wasted and haggard features. His dark brown hair hung about his face in elf-locks, his beard was untrimmed, and a fixed and stony glare like that of insanity sat in his eye. He was seated on the ground–neither bench nor stool being allowed him–with his hand supporting his chin. His gaze was fixed upon vacancy–if that can be called vacancy, which to him was filled with vivid images. His garb was not that of modern times, but consisted of a doublet and hose of rich material, wrought in the fashion of Elizabeth's days.

After remaining for some time in this musing attitude, Auriol opened the old tome before him, and began to turn over its leaves. It was full of magical disquisitions and mysterious characters, and he found inscribed on one of its earlier pages a name which instantly riveted his attention. Having vainly sought some explanation of this name in the after contents of the book, he laid it aside, and became lost in meditation. His reverie ended, he heaved a deep sigh, and turned again to the open volume lying before him, and in doing so his eye rested for the first time on his habiliments. On beholding them he started, and held out his arm to examine the sleeve more narrowly. Satisfied that he was not deceived, he arose and examined himself from head to foot. He found himself, as has been stated, attired in the garb of a gentleman of Elizabeth's time.

115

"What can this mean?" he cried. "Have I endured a long and troubled dream, during which I have fancied myself living through more than two centuries? Oh, Heaven, that it may be so! Oh, that the fearful crimes I suppose I have committed have only been enacted in a dream! Oh, that my victims are imaginary! Oh, that Ebba should only prove a lovely phantom of the night! And yet, I could almost wish the rest were real–so that she might exist. I cannot bear to think that she is nothing more than a vision, But it must be so–I have been dreaming– and what a dream it has been!–what strange glimpses it has afforded me into futurity! Methought I lived in the reigns of many sovereigns– beheld one of them carried to the block–saw revolutions convulse the kingdom–old dynasties shaken down, and new ones spring up. Fashions seem to me to have so changed, that I had clean forgotten the old ones; while my fellow-men scarcely appeared the same as heretofore. Can I be the same myself? Is this the dress I once wore? Let me seek for some proof."

And thrusting his hand into his doublet, he drew forth some tablets, and hastily examined them. They bore his name, and contained some writing, and he exclaimed aloud with joy, "This is proof enough–I have been dreaming all this while."

"The scheme works to a miracle," muttered a personage stationed at the foot of the steps springing from the doorway, and who, though concealed from view himself, was watching the prisoner with a malignant and exulting gaze.

"And yet, why am I here?" pursued Auriol, looking around. "Ah! I see how it is," he added, with a shudder; "I have been mad– perhaps am mad still. That will account for the strange delusion under which I have laboured."

"I will act upon that hint," muttered the listener.

"Of what use is memory," continued Auriol, musingly, "if things that are not, seem as if they were? If joys and sorrows which we have never endured are stamped upon the brain–if visions of scenes, and faces and events which we have never witnessed, never known, haunt us, as if they had once been familiar? But I am mad–mad!"

The listener laughed to himself.

"How else, if I were not mad, could I have believed that I had swallowed the fabled elixir vitae? And yet, is it a fable? for I am puzzled still. Methinks I am old–old–old–though I feel young, and look young. All this is madness. Yet how clear and distinct it seems! I can call to mind events in Charles the Second's time. Ha!–who told me of Charles the Second? How know I there was such a king? The reigning sovereign should be James, and yet I fancy it is George the Fourth. Oh! I am mad–clean mad!"

There was another pause, during which the listener indulged in a suppressed fit of laughter. "Would I could look forth from this dungeon," pursued Auriol, again breaking silence, "and satisfy myself of the truth or falsehood of my doubts by a view of the external world, for I am so perplexed in mind, that if I were not distracted already, they would be enough to drive me so. What dismal, terrible fancies have possessed me, and weigh upon me still–the compact with Rougemont–ha!"

"Now it comes," cried the listener.

"Oh, that I could shake off the conviction that this were not so– that my soul, though heavily laden, might still be saved! Oh, that I dared to hope this!"

"I must interrupt him if he pursues this strain," said the listener.

"Whether my crimes are real or imaginary–whether I snatched the cup of immortality from my grandsire's dying lips–whether I signed a compact with the Fiend, and delivered him a victim on each tenth year–I cannot now know; but if it is so, I deeply, deeply regret them, and would expiate my offences by a life of penance."

At this moment Rougemont, attired in a dress similar to that of the prisoner, marched up the steps, and cried, "What ho, Auriol!– Auriol Darcy!"

"Who speaks?" demanded Auriol "Ah! is it you, Fiend?"

"What, you are still in your old fancies," rejoined Rougemont. "I thought the draught I gave you last night would have amended you."

"Tell me who and what I am," cried Auriol, stupefied with astonishment; "in what age I am living; and whether I am in my right mind or not?"

"For the first, you are called Auriol Darcy," replied Rougemont; "for the second, you are living in the reign of his most Catholic Majesty James I of England, and VIth of Scotland; and for the third, I trust you will soon recover your reason."

"Amazement!" cried Auriol, striking his brow with his clenched hand. "Then I am mad."

"It's plain your reason is returning, since you are conscious of your condition," replied Rougemont; "but calm yourself, you have been subject to raging frenzies."

"And I have been shut up here for safety?" demanded Auriol.

"Precisely," observed the other. "And you are—"

"Your keeper," replied Rougemont.

"My God! what a brain mine must be!" cried Auriol. "Answer me one question–Is there such a person as Ebba Thorneycroft?"

"You have often raved about her," replied Rougemont. "But she is a mere creature of the imagination."

Auriol groaned, and sank against the wall.

"Since you have become so reasonable, you shall again go forth into the world," said Rougemont; "but the first essay must be made at night, for fear of attracting observation. I will come to you again a few hours hence. Farewell, for the present."

And casting a sinister glance at his captive, he turned upon his heel, descended the steps, and quitted the cell.

VI. Doctor Lamb Again

Night came, and the cell grew profoundly dark. Auriol became impatient for the appearance of his keeper, but hour after hour passed and he did not arrive. Worn out, at length, with doubt and bewildering speculations, the miserable captive was beset with the desire to put an end to his torments by suicide, and he determined to execute his fell purpose without delay. An evil chance seemed also to befriend him, for scarcely was the idea formed, than his foot encountered something on the ground, the rattling of which attracted his attention, and stooping to take it up, he grasped the bare blade of a knife.

"This will, at all events, solve my doubts," he cried aloud. "I will sheathe this weapon in my heart, and, if I am mortal, my woes will be ended."

As he spoke, be placed the point to his breast with the full intent to strike, but before he could inflict the slightest wound, his arm was forcibly arrested.

"Would you destroy yourself, madman?" roared a voice. "I thought your violence was abated, and that you might go forth in safety. But I find you are worse than ever."

Auriol uttered a groan and let the knife fall to the ground. The newcomer kicked it to a distance with his foot.

"You shall be removed to another chamber," he pursued, "where you can be more strictly watched."

"Take me forth oh! take me forth," cried Auriol. "It was a mere impulse of desperation, which I now repent."

"I dare not trust you. You will commit some act of insane fury, for which I myself shall have to bear the blame. When I yielded to your entreaties on a former occasion, and took you forth, I narrowly prevented you from doing all we met a mischief."

"I have no recollection of any such circumstance," returned Auriol, mournfully. "But it may be true, nevertheless. And if so, it only proves the lamentable condition to which I am reduced memory and reason gone!"

"Ay, both gone," cried the other, with an irrepressible chuckle. "Ha!" exclaimed Auriol, starring. "I am not so mad but I recognize in you the Evil Being who tempted me. I am not so oblivious as to forget our terrible interviews."

"What, you are in your lunes again!" cried Rougemont fiercely. "Nay, then I must call my assistants, and bin you."

"Let me be–let me be!" implored Auriol, "and I will offend you no more. Whatever thoughts may arise within me, I will not give utterance to them. Only take me forth."

"I came for that purpose," said Rougemont; "but I repeat, I dare not. You are not sufficiently master of yourself."

"Try me," said Auriol.

"Well," rejoined the other, "I will see what I can do to calm you."

So saying, he disappeared for a few moments, and then returning with a torch, placed it on the ground, and producing a phial, handed it to the captive.

"Drink!" he said.

Without a moment's hesitation Auriol complied.

"It seems to me rather a stimulant than a soothing potion," he remarked, after emptying the phial.

"You are in no condition to judge," rejoined the other.

And he proceeded to unfasten Auriol's chain.

"Now then, come with me," he said, "and do not make any attempt at evasion, or you will rue it."

Like one in a dream, Auriol followed his conductor down the flight of steps leading from the dungeon, and along a narrow passage. As he proceeded, he thought he heard stealthy footsteps behind him; but he never turned his head, to see whether he was really followed. In this way they reached a short steep staircase, and, mounting it, entered a vault, in which Rougemont paused, and placed the torch he had brought with him upon the floor. Its lurid glimmer partially illumined the chamber, and showed that it was built of stone. Rude benches of antique form were set about the vault, and motioning Auriol to be seated upon one of them, Rougemont sounded a silver whistle. The summons was shortly afterwards answered by the dwarf, in whose attire a new change had taken place. He was now clothed in a jerkin of grey serge, fashioned like the garments worn by the common people in Elizabeth's reign, and wore a trencher cap on his head. Auriol watched him as he timidly advanced towards Rougemont, and had an indistinct recollection of having seen him before; but could not call to mind how or where.

"Is your master a-bed?" demanded Rougemont.

"A-bed! Good lack, sir!" exclaimed the dwarf, "little of sleep; knows Doctor Lamb. He will toil at the furnace till the stars have set."

"Doctor Lamb!" repeated Auriol. "Surely I have heard that name before?"

"Very likely," replied Rougemont, "for it is the name borne by your nearest kinsman."

"How is the poor young gentleman?" asked the dwarf, glancing commiseratingly at Auriol. "My master often makes inquiries after his

121

grandson, and grieves that the state of his mind should render it necessary to confine him."

"His grandson! I–Doctor Lamb's grandson!" cried Auriol.

"In sooth are you, young sir," returned the dwarf. "Were you in your reason, you would be aware that my master's name is the same as your own–Darcy–Reginald Darcy. He assumes the name of Doctor Lamb to delude the multitude. He told you as much yourself, sweet sir, if your poor wits would enable you to recollect it."

"Am I in a dream, good fellow, tell me that?" cried Auriol, lost in amazement.

"Alack, no, sir," replied the dwarf; "to my thinking, you are wide awake. But you know, sir," he added, touching his forehead, "you have been a little wrong here, and your memory and reason are not of the clearest."

"Where does my grandsire dwell?" asked Auriol.

"Why here, sir," replied the dwarf; "and for the matter of locality, the house is situated on the south end of London-bridge."

"On the bridge–did you say on the bridge, friend?" cried Auriol.

"Ay, on the bridge–where else should it be? You would not have your grandsire live under the river?" rejoined the dwarf; "though, for ought I know, some of these vaults may go under it. They are damp enough."

Auriol was lost in reflection, and did not observe a sign that passed between the dwarf and Rougemont.

"Will it disturb Doctor Lamb if his grandson goes up to him?" said the latter, after a brief pause.

"My master does not like to be interrupted in his operations, as you know, sir," replied the dwarf, "and seldom suffers anyone, except myself, to enter his laboratory; but I will make so bold as to introduce Master Auriol, if he desires it."

"You will confer the greatest favour on me by doing so," cried Auriol, rising.

"Sit down–sit down!" said Rougemont, authoritatively. "You cannot go up till the doctor has been apprised. Remain here, while Flapdragon and I ascertain his wishes." So saying, he quitted the chamber by a farther outlet with the dwarf.

During the short time that Auriol was left alone, he found it vain to attempt to settle his thoughts, or to convince himself that he was not labouring under some strange delusion. He was aroused at length by the dwarf, who returned alone.

"Your grandsire will see you," said the mannikin.

"One word before we go," cried Auriol, seizing his arm.

"Saints! how you frighten me!" exclaimed the dwarf. "You must keep composed, or I dare not take you to my master."

"Pardon me," replied Auriol; "I meant not to alarm you. Where is the person who brought me hither?"

"What, your keeper?" said the dwarf. "Oh, he is within call. He will come to you anon. Now follow me."

And taking up the torch, he led the way out of the chamber. Mounting a spiral staircase, apparently within a turret, they came to a door, which being opened by Flapdragon, disclosed a scene that well-nigh stupefied Auriol.

It was the laboratory precisely as he had seen it above two centuries ago. The floor was strewn with alchemical implements–the table was covered with mystic parchments inscribed with cabalistic characters–the furnace stood in the corner–crucibles and cucurbites decorated the chimney-board–the sphere and brazen lamp hung from the ceiling–

the skeletons grinned from behind the chimney-corner–all was there as he had seen it before! There was also Doctor Lamb, in his loose gown of sable silk, with a square black cap upon his venerable head, and his snowy beard streaming to his girdle.

The old man's gaze was fixed upon a crucible placed upon the furnace, and he was occupied in working the bellows. He moved his head as Auriol entered the chamber, and the features became visible. It was a face never to be forgotten.

"Come in, grandson," said the old man, kindly. "Come in, and close the door after you. The draught affects the furnace–my Athanor, as we adepts term it. So you are better, your keeper tells me–much better."

"Are you Indeed living?" cried Auriol, rushing wildly towards him, and attempting to take his hand.

"Off–off!" cried the old man, drawing back as if alarmed. "You disturb my operations. Keep him calm, Flapdragon, or take him hence. He may do me a mischief."

"I have no such intention, sir," said Auriol; "indeed I have not. I only wish to be assured that you are my aged relative."

"To be sure he is, young sir," interposed the dwarf. "Why should you doubt it?"

"Oh! sir," cried Auriol, throwing himself at the old man's feet, "pity me if I am mad; but offer me some explanation, which may tend to restore me to my senses. My reason seems gone, yet I appear capable of receiving impressions from external objects. I see you, and appear to know you. I see this chamber–these alchemical implements–that furnace–these different objects–and I appear to recognize them. Am I deceived, or is this real?"

"You are not deceived, my son," replied the old man. "You have been in this room before, and you have seen me before. It would be useless to explain to you now how you have suffered from fever, and

124

what visions your delirium has produced. When you are perfectly re-stored, we will talk the matter over."

And, as he said this, he began to blow the fire anew, and watched with great apparent interest the changing colours of the liquid cucurbite placed on the furnace.

Auriol looked at him earnestly, but could not catch another glance, so intently was the old man occupied. At length he ventured to break the silence.

"I should feel perfectly convinced, if I might look forth from that window," he said.

"Convinced of what?" rejoined the old man, somewhat sharply.

"That I am what I seem," replied Auriol.

"Look forth, then," said the old man. "But do not disturb me by idle talk. There is the rosy colour in the projection for which I have been so long waiting."

Auriol then walked to the window and gazed through the tinted panes. It was very dark, and objects could only be imperfectly distinguished. Still he fancied he could detect the gleam of the river beneath him, and what seemed a long line of houses on the bridge. He also fancied he discerned other buildings, with the high roofs, the gables, and the other architectural peculiarities of the structures of Elizabeth's time. He persuaded himself, also, that he could distinguish through the gloom the venerable Gothic pile of Saint Paul's Cathedral on the other side of the water, and, as if to satisfy him that he was right, a deep solemn bell tolled forth the hour of two. After a while he returned from the window, and said to his supposed grandsire, "I am satisfied. I have lived centuries in a few nights."

VI. The Charles the Second Spaniel

IT was about two o'clock, on a charming spring day, that a stout middle-aged man, accompanied by a young person of extraordinary beauty, took up his station in front of Langham Church. Just as the clock struck the hour, a young man issued at a quick pace from a cross-street, and came upon the couple before he was aware of it. He was evidently greatly embarrassed, and would have beaten a retreat, but that was impossible. His embarrassment was in some degree shared by the young lady; she blushed deeply, but could not conceal her satisfaction at the encounter. The elder individual, who did not appear to notice the confusion of either party, immediately extended his hand to the young man, and exclaimed:

"What! Mr. Darcy, is it you? Why, we thought we had lost you, sir! What took you off so suddenly? We have been expecting you these four days, and were now walking about to try and find you. My daughter has been, terrible uneasy. Haven't you, Ebba?"

The young lady made no answer to this appeal, but east down her eyes.

"It was my intention to call, and give you an explanation of my strange conduct, today," replied Auriol. "I hope you received my letter, stating that my sudden departure was unavoidable."

"To be sure; and I also received the valuable snuff-box you were so good as to send me," replied Mr. Thorneycroft. "But you neglected to tell me how to acknowledge the gift."

"I could not give an address at the moment," said Auriol.

"Well, I am glad to find you have got the use of your arm again," observed the iron-merchant; "but I can't say you look so well as when you left us. You seem paler–eh? what do you think, Ebba?"

"Mr. Darcy looks as if he were suffering from mental anxiety rather than from bodily ailment," she replied, timidly..

"I am so," replied Auriol, regarding her fixedly. "A very disastrous circumstance has happened to me. But answer me one question: has the mysterious person in the black cloak troubled you again?"

"What mysterious person?" demanded Mr. Thorneycroft, opening his eyes.

"Never mind, father," replied Ebba. "I saw him last night," she added to Auriol. "I was sitting in the back room alone, wondering what had become of you, when I heard a tap against the window, which was partly open, and, looking up, I beheld the tall stranger. It was nearly dark, but the light of the fire revealed his malignant countenance. I don't exaggerate, when I say his eyes gleamed like those of a tiger. I was terribly frightened, but something prevented me from crying out. After gazing at me for a few moments, with a look that seemed to fascinate while it frightened me, he said–'You desire to see Auriol Darcy. I have just quitted him. Go to Langham-place tomorrow, and, as the clock strikes two, you will behold him.' Without waiting for any reply on my part, he disappeared."

"Ah, you never told me this, you little rogue!" cried Mr. Thorneycroft. "You persuaded me to come out with you, in the hope of meeting Mr. Darcy; but you did not say you were sure to find him. So you sent this mysterious gentleman to her, eh?" he added to Auriol.

"No, I did not," replied the other, gloomily.

"Indeed!" exclaimed the iron-merchant with a puzzled look.

"Oh, then I suppose he thought it might relieve her anxiety. However, since we have met, I hope you'll walk home and dine with us."

Auriol was about to decline the invitation, but Ebba glanced at him entreatingly.

"I have an engagement, but I will forgo it," he said, offering his arm to her.

And they walked along towards Oxford-street, while Mr. Thorneycroft followed a few paces behind them.

"This is very kind of you, Mr. Darcy," said Ebba. "Oh, I have been so wretched."

"I grieve to hear it," he rejoined. "I hoped you had forgotten me."

"I am sure you did not think so," she cried.

As she spoke, she felt a shudder pass through Auriol's frame.

"What ails you?" she anxiously inquired.

"I would have shunned you, if I could, Ebba," he replied; "but a fate, against which it is vain to contend, has brought us together again."

"I am glad of it," she replied; "because ever since our last interview, I have been reflecting on what you then said to me, and am persuaded you are labouring under some strange delusion, occasioned by your recent accident."

"Be not deceived, Ebba," cried Auriol. "I am under a terrible influence. I need not remind you of the mysterious individual who tapped at your window last night."

"What of him?" demanded Ebba, with a thrill of apprehension. "He it is who controls my destiny," replied Auriol.

"But what has he to do with me?" asked Ebba.

"Much, much," he replied, with a perceptible shudder.

"You terrify me, Auriol," she rejoined. "Tell me what you mean–in pity, tell me?"

Before Auriol could reply Mr. Thorneycroft stepped forward, and turned the conversation into another channel.

Soon after this, they reached the Quadrant, and were passing beneath the eastern colonnade, when Ebba's attention was attracted towards a man who was leading a couple of dogs by a string, while he had others under his arm, others again in his pocket, and another in his breast. It was Mr. Ginger.

"What a pretty little dog!" cried Ebba, remarking the Charles the Second spaniel.

"Allow me to present you with it?" said Auriol.

"You know I should value it, as coming from you," she replied, blushing deeply; "but I cannot accept it; so I will not look at it again, for fear I should be tempted."

The dog-fancier, however, noticing Ebba's admiration, held forward the spaniel, and said, "Do jist look at the pretty little creater, miss. It han't its equil for beauty. Don't be afeerd on it, miss. It's as gentle as a lamb."

"Oh! you little darling!" Ebba said, patting its sleek head and long silken ears, while it fixed its large black eyes upon her, as if entreating her to become its purchaser.

"Fairy seems to have taken quite a fancy to you miss," observed Ginger; "and she aint i' the habit o' fallin' i' love at first sight. I don't wonder at it, though for my part. I should do jist the same, if I wos in her place. Veil, now, miss, as she seems to like you, and you seem to like her, I won't copy the manners o' them 'ere fathers as has stony 'arts, and part two true lovvers. You shall have her a bargain."

"What do you call a bargain, my good man?" inquired Ebba, smiling.

"I wish I could afford to give her to you, miss," replied Ginger; "you should have her, and welcome. But I must airn a livelihood, and

Fairy is the most wallerable part o' my stock. I'll tell you wot I give for her myself, and you shall have her at a trifle beyond it. I'd scorn to take adwantage o' the likes o' you."

"I hope you didn't give too much, then, friend," replied Ebba.

"I didn't give hayf her wally–not hayf," said Ginger; "and if so be you don't like her in a month's time, I'll buy her back again from you. You'll alvays find me here–alvays. Everybody knows Mr. Ginger–that's my name, miss. I'm the only honest man in the dog-fancyin' line. Ask Mr. Bishop, the great gunmaker o' Bond-street, about me– him as the nobs call the Bishop o' Bond-street–an: he'll tell you."

"But you haven't answered the lady's question," said Auriol. "What do you ask for the dog?"

"Do you want it for yourself, sir, or for her?" inquired Ginger.

"What does it matter?" cried Auriol, angrily.

"A great deal, sir," replied Ginger; "it'll make a mater'al difference in the price. To you, she'll be five-an'-twenty guineas. To the young lady, twenty."

"But suppose I buy her for the young lady?" said Auriol.

"Oh, then, in coorse, you'll get her at the lower figure!" replied Ginger.

"I hope you don't mean to buy the dog?" interposed Mr. Thorneycroft. "The price is monstrous–preposterous."

"It may appear so to you, sir," said Ginger, "because you're ignorant o' the wally of sich a hanimal; but I can tell you it's cheap–dirt cheap. Vy, his excellency the Prooshian ambassador bought a Charley from me, t'other week, to present to a certain duchess of his acquaintance, and wot d'ye think he give for it?"

"I don't know, and I don't want to know," replied Mr. Thorney-croft, gruffly.

"Eighty guineas," said Ginger. "Eighty guineas, as I'm a livin' man, and made no bones about it neither. The dog I sold him warn't to be compared wi' Fairy."

"Stuff–stuff!" cried Mr. Thorneycroft; "I aint' to be gammoned in that way."

"It's no gammon," said Ginger. "Look at them ears, miss.–vy, they're as long as your own ringlets–and them pads–an' I'm sure you von't-ay she's dear at twenty pound."

"She's a lovely little creature, indeed," returned Ebba, again pat-ting the animal's head.

While this was passing, two men of very suspicious mien, en-sconced behind a pillar adjoining the group, were reconnoitring Auriol.

"It's him!" whispered the taller and darker of the two to his com-panion–"it's the young man ve've been lookin' for–Auriol Darcy."

"It seems like him," said the other, edging round the pillar as far as he could without exposure. "I vish he'd turn his face a leetle more this vay."

"It's him I tell you, Sandman," said the Tinker. "Ve must give the signal to our comrade."

"Vell, I'll tell you wot it is, miss," said Ginger, coaxingly, "your sveet'art–I'm sure he's your sveet'art–I can tell these things in a minnit–your sveet'art, I say, shall give me fifteen pound, and the dog's yourn. I shall lose five pound by the transaction; but I don't mind it for sich a customer as you. Fairy desarves a kind missus."

Auriol, who had fallen into a fit of abstraction, here remarked:

131

"What's that you are saying, fellow?"

"I vos a-sayin', sir, the young lady shall have the dog for fifteen pound, and a precious bargin it is," replied Ginger.

"Well, then, I close with you. Here's the money," said Auriol, taking out his purse.

"On no account, Auriol," cried Ebba, quickly. "It's too much."

"A great deal too much, Mr. Darcy," said Thorneycroft.

"Auriol and Darcy!" muttered Ginger. "Can this be the gemman ve're a-lookin' for. Vere's my two pals, I vonder? Oh, it's all right!" he added, receiving a signal from behind the pillar. "They're on the look-out, I see."

"Give the lady the dog, and take the money, man," said Auriol, sharply.

"Beg pardon, sir," said Ginger, "but hadn't I better carry the dog home for the young lady? It might meet with some accident in the vay."

"Accident!–stuff and nonsense!" cried Mr. Thorneycroft. "The rascal only wants to follow you home, that he may know where you live, and steal the dog back again. Take my advice, Mr. Darcy, and don't buy it."

"The bargain's concluded," said Ginger, delivering the dog to Ebba, and taking the money from Auriol, which, having counted, he thrust into his capacious breeches-pocket.

"How shall I thank you for this treasure, Auriol?" exclaimed Ebba, in an ecstasy of delight.

"By transferring to it all regard you may entertain for me," he replied, in a low tone.

"That is impossible," she answered.

"Well, I vote we drive away at once," said Mr. Thorneycroft. "Halloa! jarvey!" he cried, hailing a coach that was passing; adding, as the vehicle stopped, "Now get in, Ebba. By this means we shall avoid being followed by the rascal." So saying, he got into the coach. As Auriol was about to follow him, he felt a slight touch on his arm, and, turning, beheld a tall and very forbidding man by his side.

"Beg pardin, sir," said the fellow, touching his hat, "but ain't your name Mr. Auriol Darcy?"

"It is," replied Auriol, regarding him fixedly. "Why do you ask?"

"I vants a vord or two vith you in private—that's all, sir," replied the Tinker.

"Say what you have to say at once," rejoined Auriol. "I know nothing of you."

"You'll know me better by-and-by sir," said the Tinker, in a significant tone. "I must speak to you, and alone."

"If you don't go about your business, fellow, instantly, I'll give you in charge of the police," cried Auriol.

"No you von't sir—no you von't," replied the Tinker, shaking his head. And then, lowering his voice, he added, "You'll be glad to purchase my silence ven you larns wot secrets o' yourn has come to my knowledge."

"Won't you get in, Mr. Darcy?" cried Thorneycroft, whose back was towards the Tinker. "I must speak to this man," replied Auriol, "I'll come to you in the evening. Till then, farewell, Ebba." And, as the coach drove away, he added to the Tinker, "Now, rascal, what have you to say?"

"Step this vay, sir," replied the Tinker. "There's two friends o' mine as vishes to be present at our conference. Ve'd better valk into a back street."

VII. The hand, again!

Followed by Auriol, who, in his turn, was followed by Ginger and the Sandman, the Tinker directed his steps to Great Windmill-street; where he entered a public-house, called the Black Lion. Leaving his four-footed attendants with the landlord, with whom he was acquainted, Ginger caused the party to be shown into a private room, and, on entering it, Auriol flung himself into a chair, while the dog–fancier stationed himself near the door.

"Now what do you want with me?" demanded Auriol.

"You shall learn presently," replied the Tinker; "but first, it may be as vell to state, that a certain pocket-book has been found."

"Ah!" exclaimed Auriol. "You are the villains who beset me in the ruined house in the Vauxhall-road."

"Your pocket-book has been found, I tell you," replied the Tinker, "and from it ve have made the most awful diskiveries. Our werry 'air stood on end ven ve first read the shockin' particulars. What a bloodthirsty ruffian you must be! Vy, ve finds you've been i' the habit o' makin' avay with a young ooman vonce every ten years. Your last wictim wos in 1820–the last but one, in 1810–and the one before her, in 1800."

"Hangin's too good for you!" cried the Sandman; "but if ve peaches you're sartin to sving."

"I hope that pretty creater I jist see ain't to be the next victim?" said Ginger.

"Peace!" thundered Auriol. "What do you require?"

"A hundred pound each'll buy our silence," replied the Tinker. "Ve ought to have double that," said the Sandman, "for screenin' sich atterocious crimes as he has parpetrated. Ve're not werry partic'lar ourselves, but ve don't commit murder wholesale."

"Ve don't commit murder at all," said Ginger.

"You may fancy," pursued the Tinker, "that ve aint' perfectly acvainted with your history, but to prove that ve are, I'll just rub up your memory. Did you ever hear tell of a gemman as murdered Doctor Lamb, the famous halchemist o' Queen Bess's time, and, havin' drank the 'lixir vich the doctor had made for hisself, has lived ever since? Did you ever hear tell of such a person, I say?"

Auriol gazed at him in astonishment.

"What idle tale are you inventing?" he said, at length.

"It is no idle tale," replied the Tinker, boldly. "Ve can bring a vitness as'll prove the fact–a livin' vitness."

"What witness?" cried Auriol.

"Don't you rekilect the dwarf as used to serve Doctor Lamb?" rejoined the Tinker. "He's alive still; and ve calls him Old Parr, on account of his great age."

"Where is he?–what has become of him?" demanded Auriol.

"Oh, ve'll preduce him in doo time," replied the Tinker, cunningly.

"But tell me where the poor fellow is?" cried Auriol. "Have you seen him since last night? I sent him to a public-house at Kensington, but he has disappeared from it, and I can discover no traces of him."

"He'll turn up somewhere–never fear," rejoined the Tinker "But now, sir, that ve fairly understands each other, are you agreeable to our terms? You shall give us an order for the money, and ve'll undertake on our parts, not to mislest you more."

"The pocket-book must be delivered up to me if I assent," said Auriol, "and the poor dwarf must be found."

"Vy, as to that, I can scarcely promise," replied the Tinker; "there's a difficulty in the case, you see. But the pocket-book'll never be brought aginst you–you may rest assured o' that."

"I must have it, or you get nothing from me," cried Auriol.

"Here's a bit o' paper as come from the pocket-book," said Ginger. "Would you like to hear wot's written upon it? Here are the words:–'How many crimes have I to reproach myself with! How many innocents have I destroyed! And all owing to my fatal compact with–"

"Give me that paper," cried Auriol, rising and attempting to snatch it from the dog-fancier.

Just at this moment, and while Ginger retreated from Auriol, the door behind him was noiselessly opened–a hand was thrust through the chink–and the paper was snatched from his grasp. Before Ginger could turn round, the door was closed again.

"Halloa! What's that?" he cried. "The paper's gone!"

"The hand again!" cried the Sandman, in alarm. "See who's in the passage–open the door–quick!"

Ginger cautiously complied and, peeping forth, said:

"There's no one there. It must be the devil. I'll have nuffin' more to do wi' the matter."

"Poh! poh! don't be so chicken-'arted!" cried the Tinker. "But come what may, the gemman sha'n't stir till he undertakes to pay us three hundred pounds."

136

"You seek to frighten me in vain, villain," cried Auriol, upon whom the recent occurrence had not been lost. "I have but to stamp my foot, and I can instantly bring assistance that shall overpower you."

"Don't provoke him," whispered Ginger, plucking the Tinker's sleeve. "For my part, I shan't stay any longer. I wouldn't take his money." And he quitted the room.

"I'll go and see wot's the matter wi' Ginger," said the Sandman slinking after him.

The Tinker looked nervously round. He was not proof against his superstitious fears.

"Here, take this purse, and trouble me no more!" cried Auriol. The Tinker's hands clutched the purse mechanically, but he instantly laid it down again.

"I'm bad enough–but I won't sell myseff to the devil," he said.

And he followed his companions.

Left alone, Auriol groaned aloud, and covered his face with his hands. When he looked up, he found the tall man in the black cloak standing beside him. A demoniacal smile played upon his features.

"You here?" cried Auriol.

"Of course," replied the stranger. "I came to watch over your safety. You were in danger from those men. But you need not concern yourself more about them. I have your pocket-book, and the slip of paper that dropped from it. Here are both. Now let us talk on other matters. You have just parted from Ebba, and will see her again this evening."

"Perchance," replied Auriol.

"You will," rejoined the stranger, peremptorily. "Remember, your ten years' limit draws to a close. In a few days it will be at an end;

137

and if you renew it not, you will incur the penalty, and you know it to be terrible. With the means of renewal in your hands, why hesitate?"

"Because I will not sacrifice the girl," replied Auriol.

"You cannot help yourself," cried the stranger, scornfully. "I command you to bring her to me."

"I persist in my refusal," replied Auriol.

"It is useless to brave my power," said the stranger. "A moon is just born. When it has attained its first quarter, Ebba shall be mine. Till then, farewell."

And as the words were uttered, he passed through the door.

VIII. The Barber of London

Who has not heard of the Barber of London? His dwelling is in the neighbourhood of Lincoln's Inn. It is needless to particularize the street, for everybody knows the shop; that is to say, every member of the legal profession, high or low. All, to the very judges themselves, have their hair cut, or their wigs dressed by him. A pleasant fellow is Mr. Tuffnell Trigge–Figaro himself not pleasanter–and if you do not shave yourself–if you want a becoming flow imparted to your stubborn locks, or if you require a wig, I recommend you to the care of Mr. Tuffnell Trigge. Not only will he treat you well, but he will regale you with all the gossip of the court; he will give you the last funny thing of Mr. Serjeant Larkins; he will tell you how many briefs the great Mr. Skinner Fyne receives–what the Vice-Chancellor is doing; and you will own, on rising that have never spent a five minutes more agreeably. Besides, you are likely to see some noticeable characters, for Mr. Trigge's shop is quite a lounge. Perhaps you may find a young barrister who has just been "called", ordering his "first wig", and you may hear the prognostications of Mr. Trigge to his future distinction. "Ah, sir," he will say, glancing at the stolid features of the young man, "you have quite the face of the Chief Justice–quite the face of the chief–I don't recollect him ordering his first wig–that was a little before my time; but I hope to live to see you chief, sir. Quite within your reach, if you choose to apply. Sure of it, sir–quite sure." Or you may see him attending to some grave master in Chancery, and listening with profound attention to his remarks; or screaming with laughter at the jokes of some smart special pleader; or talking of the theatres, the actors and actresses, to some young attorneys, or pupils in conveyancers' chambers; for those are the sort of customers in whom Mr. Trigge chiefly delights; with them, indeed, he is great, for it is by them he has been dubbed the Barber of London. His shop is also frequented by managing clerks, barristers' clerks, engrossing clerks and others; but these are, for the most part, his private friends.

Mr. Trigge's shop is none of your spruce West end hair-cutting establishments, with magnificent mirrors on every side, in which you may see the back of your head, the front, and the side, all at once, with walls bedizened with glazed French paper, and with an ante-room full of bears'-grease, oils, creams, tooth-powders, and cut glass. No, it is a real barber's and hairdresser's shop, of the good old stamp, where you may get cut and curled for a shilling, and shaved for half the price.

True, the floor is not covered with a carpet. But what of that? It bears the imprint of innumerable customers, and is scattered over with their hair. In the window, there is an assortment of busts moulded in wax, exhibiting the triumphs of Mr. Trigge's art; and, above these, are several specimens of legal wigs. On the little counter behind the window, amid large pots of pomade, and bears'-grease, and the irons and brushes in constant use by the barber, are other bustos, done to the life, and for ever glancing amiably into the room. On the block is a judge's wig, which Mr. Trigge has just been dressing, and a little farther, on a higher block, is that of a counsel. On either side of the fireplace are portraits of Lord Eldon and Lord Lyndhurst. Some other portraits of pretty actresses are likewise to be seen. Against the counter rests a board, displaying the playbill of the evening; and near it is a large piece of emblematical crockery, indicating that bears'-grease may be had on the premises. Amongst Mr. Trigge's live-stock may be enumerated his favourite magpie, placed in a wicker cage in the window, which chatters incessantly, and knows everything its master avouches, "as well as a Christian".

And now as to Mr. Tuffnell Trigge himself. He is very tall and very thin, and holds himself so upright that he loses not an inch of his stature. His head is large and his face long, with marked, if not very striking features, charged, it must be admitted with a very self-satisfied expression. One cannot earn the appellation of the Barber of London without talent; and it is the consciousness of this talent that lends to Mr. Trigge's features their apparently conceited expression. A fringe of black whisker adorns his cheek and chin, and his black bristly hair is brushed back, so as to exhibit the prodigious expanse of his forehead. His eyebrows are elevated, as if in constant scorn.

The attire in which Mr. Trigge is ordinarily seen, consists of a black velvet waistcoat, and tight black continuations. These are protected by a white apron tied round his waist, with pockets to hold his scissors and combs; over all, he wears a short nankeen jacket, into the pockets of which his hands are constantly thrust when not otherwise employed. A black satin stock with a large bow encircles his throat, and his shirt is fastened by black enamel studs. Such is Mr. Tuffnell Trigge, yclept the Barber of London.

At the time of his introduction to the reader, Mr. Trigge had just advertised for an assistant, his present young man, Rutherford Watts, being about to leave him, and set up for himself in Canterbury. It was about two o'clock, and Mr. Trigge had just withdrawn into an inner room to take some refection, when, on returning, he found Watts occupied in cutting the hair of a middle-aged, sour-looking gentleman, who was seated before the fire. Mr. Trigge bowed to the sour-looking gentleman, and appeared ready to enter into conversation with him, but no notice being taken of his advances, he went and talked to his magpie.

While he was chattering to it, the sagacious bird screamed forth: "Pretty dear!–pretty dear!" "Ah! what's that? Who is it?" cried Trigge.

"Pretty dear!–pretty dear!" reiterated the magpie.

Upon this, Trigge looked around, and saw a very singular little man enter the shop. He had somewhat the appearance of a groom being clothed in a long grey coat, drab knees, and small top-boots. He had a large and remarkable projecting mouth, like that of a baboon, and a great shock head of black hair.

"Pretty dear!–pretty dear!" screamed the magpie.

"I see nothing pretty about him," thought Mr. Trigge. "What a strange fellow. It would puzzle the Lord Chancellor himself to say what his age might be."

The little man took off his hat, and making a profound bow to the barber, unfolded the Times newspaper, which he carried under his arm, and held it up to Trigge.

"What do you want, my little friend, eh?" said the barber.

"High wages!–high wages!" screamed the magpie.

"Is this yours, sir?" replied the little man, pointing to an advertisement in the newspaper.

"Yes, yes, that's my advertisement, friend," replied Mr. Trigge. "But what of it?"

Before the little man could answer a slight interruption occurred. While eyeing the newcomer, Watts neglected to draw forth the hot curling-irons, in consequence of which he burnt the sour-looking gentleman's forehead and singed his hair.

"Take care, sir!" cried the gentleman, furiously. "What the devil are you about?"

"Yes! take care, sir, as Judge Learmouth observes to a saucy witness," cried Trigge–"'take care, or I'll commit you!'"

"D–n Judge Learmouth!" cried the gentleman, angrily. "If I were a judge, I'd hang such a careless fellow."

"Sarve him right!" screamed Mag–"sarve him right!"

"Beg pardon, sir," cried Watts. "I'll rectify you in a minute."

"Well, my little friend," observed Trigge, "and what may be your object in coming to me, as the great conveyancer, Mr. Plodwell, observes to his clients–what may be your object?"

"You want an assistant, don't you, sir?" rejoined the little man, humbly.

"Do you apply on your own account, or on behalf of a friend?" asked Trigge.

"On my own," replied the little man.

"What are your qualifications?" demanded Trigge–"what are your qualifications?"

"I fancy I understand something of the business," replied the little man. "I was a perruquier myself, when wigs were more in fashion than they are now."

"Ha! indeed!" said Trigge, laughing. "That must have been in the last century–in Queen Anne's time–eh?"

"You have hit it exactly, sir," replied the little man. "It was in Queen Anne's time."

"Perhaps you recollect when wigs were first worn, my little Nestor," cried Mr. Trigge.

"Perfectly," replied the little man. "French periwigs were first worn in Charles the Second's time."

"You saw 'em, of course?" cried the barber, with a sneer.

"I did," replied the little man, quietly.

"Oh, he must be out of his mind," cried Trigge. "We shall have a commission de lunatico to issue here, as the Master of the Rolls would observe."

WILLIAM HARRISON AINSWORTH

"I hope I may suit you, sir," said the little man.

"I don't think you will, my friend," replied Mr. Trigge; "I don't think you will. You don't seem to have a hand for hair-dressing. Are you aware of the talent the art requires? Are you aware what it has cost me to earn the enviable title of the Barber of London? I'm as proud of that title as if I were—"

"Lord Chancellor!–Lord Chancellor!" screamed Mag.

"Precisely, Mag," said Mr. Trigge; "as if I were Lord Chancellor."

"Well, I'm sorry for it," said the little man, disconsolately.

"Pretty dear!" screamed Mag; "pretty dear!"

"What a wonderful bird you have got!" said the sour-looking gentleman, rising and paying Mr. Trigge. "I declare its answers are quite appropriate."

"Ah! Mag is a clever creature, sir–that she is," replied the barber. "I gave a good deal for her."

"Little or nothing!" screamed Mag–"little or nothing!"

"What is your name, friend?" said the gentleman, addressing the little man, who still lingered in the shop.

"Why, sir, I've had many names in my time," he replied. "At one time I was called Flapdragon–at another, Old Parr–but my real name, I believe, is Morse–Gregory Morse."

"An Old Bailey answer," cried Mr. Trigge, shaking his head.

"Flapdragon, alias Old Parr–alias Gregory Morse–alias—"

"Pretty dear!" screamed Mag.

"And you want a place?" demanded the sour-looking gentleman, eyeing him narrowly.

"Sadly," replied Morse.

"Well, then, follow me," said the gentleman, "and I'll see what can be done for you."

And they left the shop together.

IX. The Moon in the First Quarter

IN spite of his resolution to the contrary, Auriol found it impossible to resist the fascination of Ebba's society, and became a daily visitor at her father's house. Mr. Thorneycroft noticed the growing attachment between them with satisfaction. His great wish was to see his daughter united to the husband of her choice, and in the hope of smoothing the way, he let Auriol understand that he should give her a considerable marriage-portion.

For the last few days a wonderful alteration had taken place in Auriol's manner, and he seemed to have shaken off altogether the cloud that had hitherto sat upon his spirits. Enchanted by the change, Ebba indulged in the most blissful anticipations of the future.

One evening they walked forth together, and almost unconsciously directed their steps towards the river. Lingering on its banks, they gazed on the full tide, admired the glorious sunset, and breathed over and over again those tender nothings so eloquent in lovers' ears.

"Oh! how different you are from what you were a week ago," said Ebba, playfully. "Promise me not to indulge in any more of those gloomy fancies."

"I will not indulge in them if I can help it, rest assured, sweet Ebba," he replied. "But my spirits are not always under my control. I am surprised at my own cheerfulness this evening."

"I never felt so happy," she replied; "and the whole scene is in unison with my feelings. How soothing is the calm river flowing at our feet!–how tender is the warm sky, still flushed with red, though the sun has set! And see, yonder hangs the crescent moon. She is in her first quarter."

"The moon in her first quarter!" cried Auriol, in a tone of anguish. "All then is over."

"What means this sudden change?" cried Ebba, frightened by his looks.

"Oh, Ebba," he replied, "I must leave you. I have allowed myself to dream of happiness too long. I am an accursed being, doomed only to bring misery upon those who love me. I warned you on the onset, but you would not believe me. Let me go, and perhaps it may not yet be too late to save you."

"Oh no, do not leave me!" cried Ebba. "I have no fear while you are with me."

"But you do not know the terrible fate I am linked to," he said. "This is the night when it will be accomplished."

"Your moody fancies do not alarm me as they used to do, dear Auriol," she rejoined, "because I know them to be the fruit of a diseased imagination. Come, let us continue our walk," she added, taking his arm kindly.

"Ebba," he cried, "I implore you to let me go! I have not the power to tear myself away unless you aid me."

"I'm glad to hear it," she rejoined, "for then I shall hold you fast."

"You know not what you do!" cried Auriol. "Release me! oh, release me!"

"In a few moments the fit will be passed," she rejoined. "Let us walk towards the abbey."

"It is in vain to struggle against fate," ejaculated Auriol, despairingly.

And he suffered himself to be led in the direction proposed.

Ebba continued to talk, but her discourse fell upon a deaf ear, and at last she became silent too. In this way they proceeded along Millbank-street and Abingdon-street, until, turning off on the right, they found themselves before an old and partly demolished building. By this time it had become quite dark, for the moon was hidden behind a rack of clouds, but a light was seen in the upper storey of the structure, occasioned, no doubt, by a fire within it, which gave a very picturesque effect to the broken outline of the walls.

Pausing for a moment to contemplate the ruin, Ebba expressed a wish to enter it. Auriol offered no opposition, and passing through an arched doorway, and ascending a short, spiral, stone staircase, they presently arrived at a roofless chamber, which it was evident, from the implements and rubbish lying about, was about to be razed to the ground. On one side there was a large arch, partly bricked up, through which opened a narrow doorway, though at some height from the ground; With this a plank communicated, while beneath it lay a great heap of stones, amongst which were some grotesque carved heads. In the centre of the chamber was a large square opening, like the mouth of a trapdoor, from which the top of a ladder projected, and near it stood a flaming brazier, which had cast forth the glare seen from below. Over the ruinous walls on the right hung the crescent moon, now emerged from the cloud, and shedding a ghostly glimmer on the scene.

"What a strange place!" cried Ebba, gazing around with some apprehension. "It looks like a spot one reads of in romance. I wonder where that trap leads to?"

"Into the vault beneath, no doubt," replied Auriol. "But why did we come hither?"

As he spoke, there was a sound like mocking laughter, but whence arising it was difficult to say.

"Did you hear that sound?" cried Auriol.

"It was nothing but the echo of laughter from the street," she replied. "You alarm yourself without reason, Auriol."

"No, not without reason," he cried. "I am in the power of a terrible being, who seeks to destroy you, and I know that he is at hand. Listen to me, Ebba, and however strange my recital may appear, do not suppose it the ravings of a madman, but be assured it is the truth."

"Beware!" cried a deep voice, issuing apparently from the depths of the vault.

"Some one spoke," cried Ebba. "I begin to share your apprehensions; Let us quit this place." "Come, then," said Auriol.

"Not so fast," cried a deep voice.

And they beheld the mysterious owner of the black cloak barring their passage out.

"Ebba, you are mine," cried the stranger. "Auriol has brought you to me."

"It is false!" cried Auriol. "I never will yield her to you."

"Remember your compact," rejoined the stranger, with a mocking laugh.

"Oh, Auriol!" cried Ebba, "I fear for your soul. You have not made a compact with this fiend?"

"He has," replied the stranger; "and by that compact you are surrendered to me."

And, as he spoke, he advanced towards her, and enveloping her in his cloak, her cries were instantly stifled.

"You shall not go!" cried Auriol, seizing him. "Release her, or I renounce you wholly."

"Fool!" cried the stranger, "since you provoke my wrath, take your doom."

And he stamped on the ground. At this signal an arm was thrust from the trap-door, and Auriol's hand was seized with an iron grasp.

While this took place, the stranger bore his lovely burden swiftly up the plank leading to the narrow doorway in the wall, and just as he was passing through it he pointed towards the sky, and shouted with a mocking smile to Auriol––

"Behold! the moon is in her first quarter. My words are fulfilled!"

And he disappeared.

Auriol tried to disengage himself from the grasp imposed upon him in vain. Uttering ejaculations of rage and despair, he was dragged forcibly backwards into the vault.

X. The Statue at Charing-Cross

ONE morning, two persons took their way along Parliament-street and Whitehall, and, chatting as they walked, turning into the entrance of Spring-gardens, for the purpose of looking at the statue at Charing-cross. One of them was remarkable for his dwarfish stature and strange withered features. The other was a man of middle size, thin, rather elderly, and with a sharp countenance, the sourness of which was redeemed by a strong expression of benevolence He was clad in a black coat, rather rusty, but well brushed, buttoned up to the chin, black tights, short drab gaiters, and wore a white neckcloth and spectacles.

Mr. Loftus (for so he was called) was a retired merchant of moderate fortune, and lived in Abingdon-street. He was a bachelor, and therefore pleased himself; and being a bit of an antiquary, rambled about all day long in search of some object of interest. His walk, on the present occasion, was taken with that view.

"By Jove! what a noble statue that is, Morse!" cried Loftus, gazing at it. "The horse is magnificent–positively magnificent."

"I recollect when the spot was occupied by a gibbet, and when, in lieu of a statue, an effigy of the martyred monarch was placed there," replied Morse. "That was in the time of the Protectorate."

"You cannot get those dreams out of your head, Morse," said Loftus, smiling. "I wish I could persuade myself I had lived for two centuries and a half."

"Would you could have seen the ancient cross, which once stood there, erected by Edward the First to his beloved wife, Eleanor of Castile," said Morse, heedless of the other's remark. "It was much mutilated when I remember it; some of the pinnacles were broken, and the foliage defaced, but statues of the queen were still standing in the recesses; and altogether the effect was beautiful."

"It must have been charming," observed Loftus, rubbing his hands; "and, though I like the statue, I would much rather have had the old Gothic cross. But how fortunate the former escaped destruction in Oliver Cromwell's time."

"I can tell you how that came to pass, sir," replied Morse, "for I was assistant to John Rivers, the brazier, to whom the statue was sold."

"Ah! indeed!" exclaimed Loftus. "I have heard something of the story, but should like to have full particulars."

"You shall hear them, then," replied Morse. "Yon statue, which, as you know, was cast by Hubert le Sueur, in 1633, was ordered by parliament to be sold and broken to pieces. Well, my master, John Rivers, being a staunch royalist, though he did not dare to avow his principles, determined to preserve it from destruction. Accordingly, he offered a good round sum for it, and was declared the purchaser. But how to dispose of it was the difficulty. He could trust none of his men, but me whom he knew to be as hearty a hater of the Roundheads, and as loyal to the memory of our slaughtered sovereign, as himself. Well, we digged a great pit, secretly, in the cellar, whither the statue had been conveyed, and buried it. The job occupied us nearly a month; and during that time, my master collected together all the pieces of old brass he could procure. These he afterwards produced, and declared they were the fragments of the statue. But the cream of the jest was to come. He began to cast handles of knives and forks in brass, giving it out that they were made from the metal of the statue. And plenty of 'em he sold too, for the Cavaliers bought 'em as memorials of their martyred monarch, and the Roundheads as evidences of his fall. In this way he soon got back his outlay."

"Ha! ha! ha!" laughed Loftus.

"Well, in due season came the Restoration," pursued Morse; "and my master made known to King Charles the Second the treasure he had kept concealed for him. It was digged forth, placed in its old position–but I forget whether the brazier was rewarded. I rather think not."

"No matter," cried Loftus; "he was sufficiently rewarded by the consciousness of having done a noble action. But let us go and examine the sculpture on the pedestal more closely."

With this, he crossed over the road; and, taking off his hat, thrust his head through the iron railing surrounding the pedestal, while Morse, in order to point out the beauties of the sculpture with greater convenience, mounted upon a stump beside him.

"You are aware that this is the work of Grinling Gibbons, sir?" cried the dwarf.

"To be sure I am," replied Loftus–"to be sure. What fancy and gusto is displayed in the treatment of these trophies!"

"The execution of the royal arms is equally admirable," cried Morse.

"Never saw anything finer," rejoined Loftus–"never, upon my life."

Every one knows how easily a crowd is collected in London, and it cannot be supposed that our two antiquaries would be allowed to pursue their investigations unmolested. Several ragged urchins got round them, and tried to discover what they were looking at, at the same time cutting their jokes upon them. These were speedily joined by a street-sweeper, rather young in the profession, a ticket-porter, a butcher's apprentice, an old Israelitish clothes-man, a coalheaver, and a couple of charity-boys.

"My eyes!" cried the street-sweeper, "only twig these coves. If they ain't green 'uns, I'm done."

"Old Spectacles thinks he has found it all out," remarked the porter; "ve shall hear wot it all means, by-and-by."

"Pleash ma 'art," cried the Jew, "vat two funny old genelmen. I vonder vat they thinks they sees?"

"I'll tell 'ee; master," rejoined the butcher's apprentice; "they're a tryin' vich on 'em can see farthest into a millstone."

"Only think of living all my life in London, and never examining this admirable work of art before!" cried Loftus, quite unconscious that he had become the object of general curiosity.

"Look closer at it, old gem'man," cried the porter. "The nearer you get, the more you'll admire it."

"Quite true," replied Loftus, fancying Morse had spoken; "it'll bear the closest inspection."

"I say, Ned," observed one of the charity-boys to the other, "do you get over the railin'; they must ha' dropped summat inside. See what it is."

"I'm afraid o' spikin' myself, Joe," replied the other; "but just give us a lift, and I'll try." "Wot are you arter there, you young rascals?" cried the coal-heaver; "come down, or I'll send the perlice to you."

"Wot two precious guys these is!" cried a ragamuffin lad, accompanied by a bull-dog. "I've a good mind to chuck the little un' off the post, and set Tartar at him. Here, boy, here!"

"That 'ud be famous fun, indeed, Spicer!" cried another rapscallion behind him.

"Arrah! let 'em alone, will you there, you young divils!" cried an Irish bricklayer; "don't you see they're only two paiceable antiquaries."

"Oh, they're antiquaries, are they!" screamed the little street-sweeper. "Vell, I never see the likes on 'em afore; did you, Sam?"

"Never," replied the porter.

"Och, murther in Irish! ye're upsettin' me, an' all the fruits of my industry," cried an applewoman, against whom the bricklayer had run his barrow. "Divil seize you for a careless wagabone! Why don't you look where ye're going', and not dhrive into people in that way?"

"Axes pardon, Molly," said the bricklayer; "but I was so interested in them antiquaries, that I didn't observe ye."

"Antiquaries be hanged! what's such warmint to me?" cried the applewoman, furious. "You've destroyed my day's market, and bad luck to ye!"

"Well, never heed, Molly," cried the good-natured bricklayer; "I'll make it up t'ye. Pick up your apples, and you shall have a dhrop of the craiter if you'll come along wid me."

While this was passing, a stout gentleman came from the far-thest side of the statue, and perceiving Loftus, cried–"Why, brother-in-law, is that you?"

But Loftus was too much engrossed to notice him, and contin-ued to expiate upon the beauty of the trophies.

"What are you talking about, brother?" cried the stout gentle-man.

"Grinling Gibbons," replied Loftus, without turning round. "Horace Walpole said that no one before him could give to wood the airy lightness of a flower, and here he has given it to a stone."

"This may be all very fine, my good fellow," said the stout gen-tleman, seizing him by the shoulder, "but don't you see the crowd you're collecting round you? You'll be mobbed presently."

"Why, how the devil did you come here, brother Thorneycroft?" cried Loftus, at last recognizing him.

"Come along, and I'll tell you," replied the iron-merchant, drag-ging him away, while Morse followed closely behind them. "I'm so glad to have met you," pursued Thorneycroft, as soon as they were clear of the mob; "you'll be shocked to hear what has happened to your niece, Ebba."

"Why, what has happened to her?" demanded Loftus. "You alarm me. Out with it at once. I hate to be kept in suspense."

"She has left me," replied Thorneycroft–"left her old indulgent father–run away."

"Run away!" exclaimed Loftus. "Impossible! I'll not believe it–even from your lips."

"Would it were not so!–but it is, alas! too true," replied Thor-neycroft, mournfully. "And the thing was so unnecessary, for I would

153

gladly have given her to the young man. My sole hope is that she has not utterly disgrace'd herself."

"No, she is too high principled for that," cried Loftus. "Rest easy on that score. But with whom has she run away?"

"With a young man named Auriol Darcy," replied Thorneycroft. "He was brought to my house under peculiar circumstances."

"I never heard of him," said Loftus.

"But I have," interposed Morse. "I've known him these two hundred years."

"Eh day! who's this?" cried Thorneycroft.

"A crack-brained little fellow, whom I've engaged as valet," replied Loftus. "He fancies he was born in Queen Elizabeth's time."

"It's no fancy," cried Morse. "I am perfectly acquainted with Auriol Darcy's history. He drank of the same elixir as myself."

"If you know him, can you give us a clue to find him?" asked Thorneycroft.

"I am sorry I cannot," replied Morse. "I only saw him for a few minutes the other night, after I had been thrown into the Serpentine by the tall man in the black cloak."

"What's that you say?" cried Thorneycroft, quickly. "I have heard Ebba speak of a tall man in a black cloak having some mysterious connection with Auriol. I hope that person has nothing to do with her disappearance."

"I shouldn't wonder if he had," replied Morse. "I believe that black gentleman to be—"

"What!—who?" demanded Thorneycroft.

"Neither more nor less than the devil," replied Morse, mysteriously.

"Pshaw! poh!" cried Loftus. "I told you the poor fellow was half cracked."

At this moment, a roguish-looking fellow, with red whiskers and hair, and clad in a velveteen jacket with ivory buttons, who had been watching the iron-merchant at some distance, came up, and touching his hat, said, "Mr. Thorneycroft, I believe?"

"My name is Thorneycroft, fellow!" cried the iron-merchant, eyeing him askance. "And your name, I fancy, is Ginger?"

"Exactly, sir," replied the dog-fancier, again touching his hat, "ex-actly. I didn't think you would rekilect me, sir. I bring you some news of your darter."

"Of Ebba!" exclaimed Thorneycroft, in a tone of deep emotion. "I hope your news is good." "I wish it wos better, for her sake as well as yours, sir," replied the dog-fancier, gravely; "but I'm afeerd she's in werry bad hands."

"That she is, if she's in the hands o' the black gentleman," observed Morse.

"Vy, Old Parr, that ain't you?" cried Ginger, gazing at him in astonishment. "Vy, 'ow you are transmogrified, to be sure!"

"But what of my daughter?" cried Thorneycroft; "where is she? Take me to her, and you shall be well rewarded."

"I'll do my best to take you to her, and without any reward, sir," replied Ginger, "for my heart bleeds for the poor young creater. As I said afore, she's in dreadful bad hands."

"Do you allude to Mr. Auriol Darcy?" cried Thorneycroft.

"No, he's as much a wictim of this infernal plot as your darter," replied Ginger; "I thought him quite different at first–but I've altered my mind entirely since some matters has come to my knowledge."

"You alarm me greatly by these dark hints," cried Thorneycroft. "What is to be done?"

"I shall know in a few hours," replied Ginger. "I ain't got the exact clue yet. But come to me at eleven o'clock tonight, at the Turk's Head, at the back o' Shoreditch Church, and I'll put you on the right scent. You must come alone."

"I should wish this gentleman, my brother-in-law, to accompany me," said Thorneycroft.

"He couldn't help you," replied Ginger. "I'll take care to have plenty of assistance. It's a dangerous bus'ness, and can only be managed in a sartin way, and by a sartin person, and he'd object to any von but you. Tonight, at eleven! Good by, Old Parr. We shall meet again ere long."

And without a word more, he hurried away.

XI Preparations

On that same night, at the appointed hour, Mr. Thorneycroft repaired to Shoreditch, and entering a narrow street behind the church, speedily discovered the Turk's Head, at the door of which a hackney-coach was standing. He was shown by the landlord into a small back room, in which three men were seated at a small table, smoking, and drinking gin and water, while a fourth was standing near the fire, with his back towards the door. The latter was a tall powerfully-built man, wrapped in a rough great-coat, and did not turn round on the iron-merchant's entrance.

"You are punctual, Mr. Thorneycroft," said Ginger, who was one of the trio at the table; "and I'm happy to say, I've arranged everythin' for you, sir. My friends are ready to undertake the job. Only they von't do it on quite sich easy terms as mine."

156

The Tinker and the Sandman coughed slightly, to intimate their entire concurrence in Mr. Ginger's remark.

"As I said to you this mornin', Mr. Thorneycroft," pursued Ginger, "this is a difficult and a dangerous bus'ness; and there's no knowin' wot may come on it. But it's your only chance o' recoverin' your darter."

"Yes, it's your only chance," echoed the Tinker.

"Ve're about to risk our precious lives for you, sir," said the Sandman; "so, in coorse, ve expects a perportionate revard."

"If you enable me to regain my daughter, you shall not find me ungrateful," rejoined the iron-merchant.

"I must have a hundred pounds," said the Tinker–"that's my lowest."

"And mine, too," said the Sandman.

"I shall take nuffin' but the glory, as I said afore," remarked Ginger. "I'm sworn champion o' poor distressed young damsils; but my friends must make their own bargins."

"Well, I assent," returned Mr. Thorneycroft; "and the sooner we set out the better."

"Are you armed?" asked Ginger.

"I have a brace of pistols in my pocket," replied Thorneycroft.

"All right, then–ve've all got pops and cutlashes," said Ginger. "So let's be off."

As he spoke, the Tinker and Sandman arose; and the man in the rough great-coat, who had hitherto remained with his back to them, turned round. To the iron-merchant's surprise, he perceived that the face of this individual was covered with a piece of black crepe.

"Who is this!" he demanded with some misgiving.

"A friend," replied Ginger. "Vithout him ve could do nuffin'. His name is Reeks, and he is the chiefman in our enterprise."

"He claims a reward too, I suppose?" said Thorneycroft.

"I will tell you what reward I claim, Mr. Thorneycroft," rejoined Reeks, in a deep stern tone, "when all is over. Meantime, give me your solemn pledge, that whatever you may behold tonight, you will not divulge it."

"I give it," replied the iron-merchant, "provided always—"

"No provision, sir," interrupted the other, quickly. "You must swear to keep silence unconditionally, or I will not move a foot-step with you; and I alone can guide you where your daughter is detained."

"Svear, sir; it is your only chance," whispered Ginger.

"Well, if it must be, I do swear to keep silence," rejoined Mr. Thorneycroft; "but your proceedings appear very mysterious."

"The whole affair is mysterious," replied Reeks. "You must also consent to have a bandage passed over your eyes when you get into the coach."

"Anything more?" asked the iron-merchant.

"You must engage to obey my orders, without questioning, when we arrive at our destination," rejoined Reeks. "Otherwise, there is no chance of success."

"Be it as you will," returned Thorneycroft, "I must perforce agree."

"All then is clearly understood," said Reeks, "and we can now set out."

Upon this, Ginger conducted Mr. Thorneycroft to the coach, and as soon as the latter got into it, tied a handkerchief tightly over his eyes. In this state Mr. Thorneycroft heard the Tinker and the Sandman take their places near him, but not remarking the voice of Reeks, concluded that he must have got outside.

The next moment, the coach was put in motion, and rattled over the stones at a rapid pace. It made many turns; but at length proceeded steadily onwards, while from the profound silence around, and the greater freshness of the air, Mr. Thorneycroft began to fancy they had gained the country. Not a word was spoken by anyone during the ride.

After a while, the coach stopped, the door was opened, and Mr. Thorneycroft was helped out. The iron-merchant expected his bandage would now be removed, but he was mistaken, for Reeks, taking his arm, drew him along at a quick pace. As they advanced, the iron-merchant's conductor whispered him to be cautious, and, at the same time, made him keep close to a wall. A door was presently opened, and as soon as the party had passed through it, closed.

The bandage was then removed from Thorneycroft's eyes, and he found himself in a large and apparently neglected garden. Though the sky was cloudy, there was light enough to enable him to distinguish that they were near an old dilapidated mansion.

"We are now arrived," said Reeks, to the iron-merchant, "and you will have need of all your resolution."

"I will deliver her, or perish in the attempt," said Thorneycroft, taking out his pistols. The others drew their cutlasses.

"Now then, follow me," said Reeks, "and act as I direct."

With this he struck into an alley formed by thick hedges of privet, which brought them to the back part of the house. Passing through a door, he entered the yard, and creeping cautiously along the wall, reached a low window, which he contrived to open without noise. He then passed through it, and was followed by the others.

XII. The Chamber of Mystery

We shall now return to the night of Ebba's seizure by the mysterious stranger. Though almost deprived of consciousness by terror, the poor girl could distinguish, from the movements of her captor, that she was borne down a flight of steps, or some steep descent, and then for a considerable distance along level ground. She was next placed in a carriage, which was driven with great swiftness, and though it was impossible to conjecture in what direction she was conveyed, it seemed to her terrified imagination as if she were hurried down a precipice, and she expected every moment to be dashed in pieces. At length, the vehicle stopped, and she was lifted out of it, and carried along a winding passage; after which, the creaking of hinges announced that a door was opened. Having passed through it, she was deposited on a bench, when, fright over-mastering her, her senses completely forsook her.

On recovering, she found herself seated on a fauteuil covered with black velvet, in the midst of a gloomy chamber of vast extent, while beside her, and supporting her from falling, stood the mysterious and terrible stranger. He held a large goblet filled with some potent liquid to her lips, and compelled her to swallow a portion of it. The powerful stimulant revived her, but, at the same time, produced a strange excitement, against which she struggled with all her power. Her persecutor again held the goblet towards her, while a sardonic smile played upon his features.

"Drink!" he cried; "it will restore you, and you have much to go through."

Ebba mechanically took the cup, and raised it to her lips, but noticing the stranger's glance of exaltation, dashed it to the ground.

"You have acted foolishly," he said, sternly; "the potion would have done you good."

Withdrawing her eyes from his gaze, which she felt exercise and irresistible influence over her, Ebba gazed fearfully round the chamber.

It was vast and gloomy, and seemed like the interior of a sepulchre–the walls and ceiling being formed of black marble, while the floor was paved with the same material. Not far from where she sat, on an estrade, approached by a couple of steps, stood a table covered with black velvet, on which was placed an immense lamp, fashioned like an imp supporting a cauldron on his outstretched wings. In this lamp were several burners, which cast a lurid light throughout the chamber. Over it hung a cap equally fantastically fashioned. A dagger, with a richly wrought hilt, was stuck into the table; and beside it lay a strangely shaped mask, an open book, an antique inkstand, and a piece of parchment, on which some characters were inscribed. Opposite these stood a curiously carved ebony chair.

At the lower end of the room, which was slightly elevated above the rest, hung a large black curtain; and on the step, in front of it, were placed two vases of jet.

"What is behind that curtain?" shudderingly demanded Ebba of her companion.

"You will see anon," he replied. "Meanwhile, seat yourself on that chair, and glance at the writing on the scroll."

Ebba did not move, but the stranger took her hand, and drew her to the seat.

"Read what is written on that paper," he cried, imperiously.

Ebba glanced at the document, and a shudder passed over her frame.

"By this," she cried, "I surrender myself, soul and body, to you?"

"You do," replied the stranger.

"I have committed no crime that can place me within the power of the Fiend," cried Ebba, falling upon her knees. "I call upon Heaven for protection! Avaunt!"

161

As the words were uttered, the cap suddenly fell upon the lamp, and the chamber was buried in profound darkness. Mocking laughter rang in her ears, succeeded by wailing cries inexpressibly dreadful to hear.

Ebba continued to pray fervently for her own deliverance, and for that of Auriol. In the midst of her supplications she was aroused by strains of music in the most exquisite sweetness, proceeding apparently from behind the curtain, and while listening to these sounds she was startled by a deafening crash as if a large gong had been stricken. The cover of the lamp was then slowly raised, and the burners blazed forth as before, while from the two vases in front of the curtain arose clouds of incense, filling the chamber with stupifying fragrance.

Again the gong was stricken, and Ebba looked round towards the curtain. Above each vase towered a gigantic figure, wrapped in a long black cloak, the lower part of which was concealed by the thick vapour. Hoods, like the cowls of monks, were drawn over the heads of these grim and motionless figures; mufflers enveloped their chins, and they wore masks, from the holes of which gleamed eyes of unearthly brightness. Their hands were crossed upon their breasts. Between them squatted two other spectral forms, similarly cloaked, hooded, and masked, with their gleaming eyes fixed upon her, and their skinny fingers pointing derisively at her.

Behind the curtain was placed a strong light, which showed a wide staircase of black marble, leading to some upper chamber, and at the same time threw the reflection of a gigantic figure upon the drapery, while a hand, the finger of which pointed towards her, was thrust from an opening between its folds.

Forcibly averting her gaze, Ebba covered her eyes with her hands, but looking up again after a brief space, beheld an ebon door at the side revolve upon its hinges, and give entrance to three female figures, robed in black, hooded and veiled, and having their hands folded, in a melancholy manner, across their breasts. Slowly and noiselessly advancing, they halted within a few paces of her.

"Who, and what are ye?" she cried, wild with terror.

162

"The victims of Auriol!" replied the figure on the right. "As we are, such will you be ere long."

"What crime have you committed?" demanded Ebba.

"We have loved him," replied the second figure.

"Is that a crime?" cried Ebba. "If so, I am equally culpable with you."

"You will share our doom," replied the third figure.

"Heaven have mercy upon me!" exclaimed the agonized girl, dropping upon her knees.

At this moment a terrible voice from behind the curtain exclaimed—

"Sign, or Auriol is lost for ever."

"I cannot yield my soul, even to save him," cried Ebba distractedly.

"Witness his chastisement, then," cried the voice.

And as the words were uttered, a side door was opened on the opposite side, and Auriol was dragged forth from it by two masked personages, who looked like familiars of the Inquisition.

"Do not yield to the demands of this fiend, Ebba!" cried Auriol, gazing at her distractedly.

"Will you save him before he is cast, living, into the tomb?" cried the voice.

And at the words, a heavy slab or marble rose slowly from the floor near where Ebba sat, and disclosed a dark pit beneath.

Ebba gazed into the abyss with indescribable terror.

"There he will be immured, unless you sign," cried the voice; "and, as he is immortal, he will endure an eternity of torture."

"I cannot save him so, but I may precede him," cried Ebba. And throwing her hands aloft, she flung herself into the pit.

A fearful cry resounded through the chamber. It broke from Auriol, who vainly strove to burst from those who held him, and precipitate himself after Ebba.

Soon after this, and while Auriol was gazing into the abyss, a tongue of blue flame arose from it, danced for a moment in the air, and then vanished. No sooner was it gone than a figure, shrouded in black habiliments, and hooded and muffled up like the three other female forms, slowly ascended from the vault, apparently without support, and remained motionless at its brink.

"Ebba!" exclaimed Auriol, in a voice of despair. "Is it you?"

The figure bowed its head, but spoke not.

"Sign!" thundered the voice. "Your attempt at self-destruction has placed you wholly in my power. Sign!"

At this injunction, the figure moved slowly towards the table, and, to his unspeakable horror, Auriol beheld it take up the pen and write upon the parchment. He bent forward, and saw that the name inscribed thereon was EBBA THORNEYCROFT.

The groan to which he gave utterance was echoed by a roar of diabolical laughter.

The figure then moved slowly away, and ranged itself with the other veiled forms.

"All is accomplished," cried the voice. "Away with him!"

On this, a terrible clangour was heard; the lights were extinguished; and Auriol was dragged through the doorway from which he had been brought forth.

A Night in Rome

The Pope was saying the high, high mass.
All on Saint Peter's day;
With the power to him given by the saints in heaven.
To wash men's sins away.

The Pope he was saying the blessed mass.
And the people kneel'd around;
And from each man's soul his sins did pass.
As he kissed the holy ground.

The Grey Brother

I. Santa Maria Maggiore

Chancing to be in Rome in the August of 1830, I visited the gorgeous church of Santa Maria Maggiore during the celebration of the anniversary of the Holy Assumption.

It was a glorious sight to one unaccustomed to the imposing religious ceremonials of the Romish church, to witness all the pomp and splendour displayed at this high solemnity–to gaze down that glittering pile, and mark the various ecclesiastical dignitaries, each in their peculiar and characteristic costume, employed in the ministration of their sacred functions, and surrounded by a wide semicircle of the papal guards, so stationed to keep back the crowd, and who, with their showy scarlet attire and tall halberds, looked like the martial figures we see in the sketches of Callot. Nor was the brilliant effect of this picture diminished by the sumptuous framework in which it was set. Overhead flamed a roof resplendent with burnished gold; before me rose a canopy supported by pillars of porphyry, and shining with many-coloured stones; while on either hand were chapels devoted to some noble house, and boasting each the marble memorial of a pope.

Melodious masses proper to the service were ever and anon chanted by the papal choir, and overpowering perfume was diffused around by a hundred censers.

Subdued by the odours, the music, and the spectacle, I sank into a state of dreamy enthusiasm, during a continuance of which I almost fancied myself a convert to the faith of Rome, and surrendered myself unreflectingly to an admiration of its errors. As I gazed among the surrounding crowd, the sight of so many prostrate figures, all in attitudes of deepest devotion, satisfied me of the profound religious impression of the ceremonial. As elsewhere; this feeling was not universal; and, as elsewhere, likewise, more zeal was exhibited by the lower than the higher classes of society; and I occasionally noted amongst the latter the glitter of an eye or the flutter of a bosom, not altogether agitated; I suspect; by holy aspirations. Yet me thought, on the whole, I had never seen such abandonment of soul, such prostration of spirit, in my own colder clime, and during the exercise of my own more chastened creed, as that which in several instances I now beheld; and I almost envied the poor maiden near me, who, abject upon the earth, had washed away her sorrows, and perhaps her sins, in contrite tears.

As such thoughts swept through my mind, I felt a pleasure in singling out particular figures and groups which interested me, from their peculiarity of costume, or from their devotional fervour. Amongst others, a little to my left, I remarked a band of mountaineers from Calabria, for such I judged them to be from their wild and picturesque garb. Deeply was every individual of this little knot of peasantry impressed by the ceremonial. Every eye was humbly cast down; every knee bent; every hand was either occupied in grasping the little crucifix suspended from its owner's neck, in telling the beads of his rosary, or fervently crossed upon his bare and swarthy breast.

While gazing upon this group, I chanced upon an individual whom I had not hitherto noticed; and who now irresistibly attracted my attention. Though a little removed from the Calabrian mountaineers, and reclining against the marble walls of the church, he evidently belonged to the same company; at least, so his attire seemed to indicate, though the noble cast of his countenance was far superior to that of his comrades. He was an old man, with a face of the fine antique Roman stamp–a bold outline of prominent nose, rugged and imperious brow, and proudly-cut chin. His head and chin, as well as his naked breast, were frosted over with the snowy honours of many winters, and their hoar appearance contrasted strikingly with the tawny hue of a skin almost as dark and as lustrous as polished oak. Peasant as he was, there was something of grandeur and majesty in this old man's demeanour and physiognomy. His head declined backwards, so as completely to expose his long and muscular throat. His arms hung listlessly by his side; one hand drooped upon the pavement, the other was placed within his breast: his eyes were closed. The old man's garb was of the coarsest fabric; he wore little beyond a shirt, a loose vest, a sort of sheep-skin cloak, and canvas leggings bound around with leathern thongs. His appearance, however, was above his condition; he became his rags as proudly as a prince would have become his ermined robe.

The more I scrutinised the rigid lines of this old man's countenance, the more I became satisfied that many singular, and perhaps not wholly guiltless, events were connected with his history. The rosary was in his hand–the cross upon his breast–the beads were untold–the crucifix unclasped–no breath of prayer passed his lips. His face was turned heavenward, but his eyes were closed,–he dared not open them. Why did he come thither, if he did not venture to pray Why did he assume a penitential attitude, if he felt no penitence?

So absorbed was I in the perusal of the workings of this old man's countenance, as to be scarcely conscious that the service of high mass was concluded, and the crowd within the holy pile fast dispersing. The music was hushed, the robed prelates and their train had disappeared, joyous dames were hastening along the marble aisles to their equipages; all, save a few kneeling figures near the chapels, were departing; and the old man, aware, from the stir and hum prevailing around, that the ceremonial was at an end, arose, stretched out his arm to one of his comrades, a youth who had joined him, and prepared to follow the concourse.

Was he really blind? Assuredly not. Besides, he did not walk like as one habituated to the direst calamity that can befall our nature. He staggered in his gait, and reeled to and fro. Yet wherefore did he not venture to unclose his eyes within the temple of the Most High? What would I not have given to be made acquainted with his history! For I felt that it must be a singular one. I might satisfy my curiosity at once. He was moving slowly forward, guided by his comrade. In a few seconds it would be too late–he would have vanished from my sight. With hasty footsteps I followed him down the church, and laid my hand, with some violence, upon his shoulder.

The old man started at the touch, and turned. Now, indeed, his eyes were opened wide, and flashing full upon me,–and such eyes! Heretofore I had only dreamed of such. Age had not quenched their lightning, and I quailed beneath the fierce glances which he threw upon me. But if I was, at first, surprised at the display of anger which I had called forth in him, how much more was I astonished to behold the whole expression of his countenance suddenly change. His eyes continued fixed upon mine as if I had been a basilisk. Apparently he could not avert them; while his whole frame shivered with emotion. I advanced towards him; he shrank backwards, and, but for the timely aid of his companion, would have fallen upon the pavement.

At a loss to conceive in what way I could have occasioned him so much alarm, I rushed forward to the assistance of the old man, when his son, for such it subsequently appeared he was, rudely repelled me, and thrust his hand into his girdle; as if to seek for means to prevent further interference.

Meanwhile the group had been increased by the arrival of a third party, attracted by the cry the old man had uttered in falling. The new comer was an Italian gentleman, somewhat stricken in year; of stern and stately deportment, and with something sinister and forbidding in his aspect. He was hastening towards the old man, but he suddenly stopped, and was about to retire when he encountered my gaze. As our eyes met he started; and a terror, as sudden and lively as that exhibited by the old man, was at once depicted in his features.

My surprise was now beyond all bounds, and I continued for some moments speechless with astonishment. Not a little of the inexplicable awe which affected the old man and the stranger was communicated to myself. Altogether, we formed a mysterious and terrible triangle of which each side bore some strange and unintelligible relation to the other.

The new comer first recovered his composure, though not without an effort. Coldly turning his heel upon me, he walked towards the old man, and shook him forcibly. The latter shrank from his grasp, and endeavoured to avoid him; but it was impossible. The stranger whispered a few words in his ear, of which, from his gestures being directed towards myself, I could guess the import. The old man replied. His action in doing so was that of supplication and despair. The stranger retorted in a wild and vehement manner, and even stamped his foot upon the ground; but the old man still continued to cling to the knees of his superior.

"Weak, superstitious fool!" at length exclaimed the stranger, "I will waste no more words upon thee. Do, or say, what thou wilt; but beware!" And spurning him haughtily back with his foot, he strode away.

The old man's reverend head struck against the marble floor. His temple was cut open by the fall, and blood gushed in torrents from the wound. Recovering himself, he started to his feet–a knife was instantly in his hand, and he would have pursued and doubtless slain his aggressor, if he had not been forcibly withheld by his son, and by a priest who had joined them.

"Maledizione!" exclaimed the old man–"a blow from him–from that hand! I will stab him, though he were at the altar's foot; though he had a thousand lives, each should pay for it. Release me, Paolo! release me! for, by Heaven! he dies!"

"Peace, father!" cried the son, still struggling with him.

"Thou art not my son, to hinder my revenge!" shouted the enraged father. "Dost not see this blood–my blood–thy father's blood?– and thou holdest me back? Thou shouldst have struck him to the earth for the deed–but he was a noble, and thou daredst not lift thy hand against him!"

"Wouldst thou have had me slay him in this holy place?" exclaimed Paolo, reddening with anger and suppressed emotion.

"No, no," returned the old man, in an altered voice; "not here, not here, though 'twere but just retribution. But I will find other means of vengeance. I will denounce him–I will betray all, though it cost me my own life! He shall die by the hands of the common executioner;– there is one shall testify for me!" And he pointed to me.

Again I advanced towards him.

"If thou hast aught to disclose pertaining to the Holy Church, I am ready to listen to thee, my son," said the priest; "but reflect well ere thou bringest any charge thou mayest not be able to substantiate against one who stands so high in her esteem as him thou wouldst accuse."

The son gave his father a meaning look, and whispered somewhat in his ear. The old man became suddenly still.

"Right, right," said he; "I have bethought me. 'Twas but a blow. He is wealthy, I am poor; there is no justice for the poor in Rome."

"My purse is at your service," said I, interfering; "you shall have my aid."

"Your aid!" echoed the old man, staring at me; "will you assist me, signor?"

"I will."

"Enough. I may claim fulfilment of your promise."

"Stop, old man," I said; "answer me one question ere you depart. Whence arose your recent terrors."

"You shall know hereafter, signor," he said; "I must now be gone. We shall meet again. Follow me not," he continued, seeing I was bent upon obtaining further explanation of the mystery. "You will learn nothing now, and only endanger my safety. Addio, signor." And with hasty steps he quitted the church, accompanied by his son.

"Who is that old man?" I demanded of the priest.

"I am as ignorant as yourself," he replied, "but he must be looked to; he talks threateningly." And he beckoned to an attendant.

"Who was he who struck him?" was my next inquiry.

"One of our wealthiest nobles," he replied, "and an assured friend of the church. We could ill spare him. Do not lose sight of them," he added to the attendant, "and let the sbirri track them to their haunts. They must not be suffered to go forth to-night. A few hours' restraint will cool their hot Calabrian blood."

"But the name of the noble, father?" I said, renewing my inquiries.

"I must decline further questioning," returned the priest, coldly. "I have other occupation; and meanwhile it will be well to have these stains effaced, which may else bring scandal on these holy walls. You will excuse me, my son." So saying, he bowed and retired.

I made fruitless inquiries for the old man at the door of the church. He was gone; none of the bystanders who had seen him go forth knew whither.

Stung by curiosity, I wandered amid the most unfrequented quarters of Rome throughout the day, in the hope of meeting with the old Calabrian, but in vain. As, however, I entered the court-yard of my hotel, I fancied I discovered, amongst the lounging assemblage gathered round the door, the dark eyes of the younger mountaineer. In this I might have been mistaken. No one answering to his description had been seen near the house.

II. The Marchesa

Une chose ténébreuse fait par des hommes ténébreux.

–Lucrece Borgia.

On the same night I bent my steps towards the Colosseum; and, full of my adventure of the morning, found myself, not without apprehension, involved within its labyrinthine passages. Accompanied by a monk, who, with a small horn lantern in his hand, acted as my guide, I fancied that, by its uncertain light, I could discover stealthy figures lurking within the shades of the ruin.

Whatever suspicions I might entertain, I pursued my course in silence. Emerging from the vomitorio, we stood upon the steps of the colossal amphitheatre. The huge pile was bathed in rosy moonlight, and reared itself in serene majesty before my view.

While indulging in a thousand speculations, occasioned by the hour and the spot, I suddenly perceived a figure on a point of the ruin immediately above me. Nothing but the head was visible; but that was placed in bold relief against the beaming sky of night, and I recognised it at once. No nobler Roman head had ever graced the circus when Rome was in her zenith. I shouted to the old Calabrian, for he it was I beheld. Almost ere the sound had left my lips, he had disappeared. I made known what I had seen to the monk. He was alarmed–urged our instant departure, and advised me to seek the assistance of the sentinel stationed at the entrance to the pile. To this proposal I assented; and, having descended the vasty steps and crossed the open arena, we arrived, without molestation, at the doorway.

The sentinel had allowed no one to pass him. He returned with me to the circus; and, after an ineffectual search amongst the ruins, volunteered his services to accompany me homewards through the Forum. I declined his offer, and shaped my course towards a lonesome vicolo on the right. This was courting danger; but I cared not, and walked slowly forward through the deserted place.

Scarcely had I proceeded many paces, when I heard footsteps swiftly approaching; and, ere I could turn round, my arms were seized from behind, and a bandage was passed across my eyes. All my efforts at liberation were unavailing; and, after a brief struggle, I remained passive.

"Make no noise," said a voice which I knew to be that of the old man, "and no harm shall befall you. You must come with us. Ask no questions, but follow."

I suffered myself to be led, without further opposition whithersoever they listed. We walked for it might be half an hour, much beyond the walls of Rome. I had to scramble through many ruins and frequently stumbled over inequalities of ground. I now felt the fresh breeze of night blowing over the wide campagna, and my conductors moved swiftly onwards as we trod on its elastic turf.

At length they came to a halt. My bandage was removed, and I beheld myself beneath the arch of an aqueduct, which spanned the moonlit plain. A fire was kindled beneath the arch, and the ruddy flame licked its walls. Around the blaze were grouped the little band of peasantry I had beheld within the church, in various and picturesque attitudes. They greeted my conductors on their arrival, and glanced inquisitively at me, but did not speak to me. The elder Calabrian, whom they addressed as Cristofano, asked for a glass of aqua vitae, which he handed respectfully to me. I declined the offer, but he pressed it upon me.

"You will need it, Signor," he said; "you have much to do to-night. You fear, perhaps, it is drugged. Behold!" And he drank it off.

I could not, after this, refuse his pledge. "And now, signor," said the old man, removing to a little distance from the group, "may I crave a word with you–your name?"

As I had no reason for withholding it, I told him how I was called.

"Hum! Had you no relation of the name of—"

"None whatever." And I sighed, for I thought of my desolate condition.

"Strange!" he muttered; adding, with a grim smile, "but, however, likenesses are easily accounted for."

"What likenesses?" I asked. "Whom do I resemble? and what is the motive of your inexplicable conduct?"

"You shall hear," he replied, frowning gloomily. "Step aside, and let us get within the shade of these arches, out of the reach of yonder listeners. The tale I have to tell is for your ears alone."

I obeyed him; and we stood beneath the shadow of the aqueduct.

"Years ago," began the old man, "an Englishman, in all respects resembling yourself; equally well-favoured in person, and equally young, came to Rome, and took up his abode within the eternal city. He was of high rank in his own country, and was treated with the distinction due to his exalted station here. At that time I dwelt with the Marchese di—. I was his confidential servant–his adviser–his friend. I had lived with his father–carried him as an infant–sported with him as a boy–loved and served him as a man. Loved him, I say; for, despite his treatment of me, I loved him then as much as I abhor him now. Well! signor, to my story. If his youth had been profligate, his manhood was not less depraved; it was devoted to cold, calculating libertinism. Soon after he succeeded to the estates and title of his father, he married. That he loved his bride, I can scarcely believe; for, though he was wildly jealous of her, he was himself unfaithful, and she knew it. In Italy, revenge, in such cases; is easily within a woman's power; and, for aught I know, the marchesa might have meditated retaliation. My lord, however, took the alarm, and thought fit to retire to his villa without the city, and for a time remained secluded within its walls. It was at this crisis that the Englishman I have before mentioned arrived in Rome. My lady, who mingled little with the gaieties of the city, had not beheld him; but she could not have been unacquainted with him by report, as every tongue was loud in his praises. A rumour of his successes with other dames had reached my lord; nay, I have reason to believe that he had been thwarted by the handsome Englishman in some other quarter, and he sedulously prevented their meeting. An interview, however, did take place between them, and in an unexpected manner. It was the custom then, as now, upon particular occasions, to drive, during the heats of summer, within the Piazza Navona, which is flooded with water. One evening the marchesa drove thither: she was unattended, except by myself. Our carriage happened to be stationed near that of the young Englishman."

"The marchesa was beautiful, no doubt?" I said, interrupting him.

"Most beautiful!" he replied; "and so your countryman seemed to think, for he was lost in admiration of her. I am not much versed in the language of the eyes, but his were too eloquent and expressive not to be understood. I watched my mistress narrowly. It was evident from her glowing cheek, though her eyes were cast down, that she was not insensible to his regards. She turned to play with her dog, a lovely little greyhound, which was in the carriage beside her, and patted it carelessly with the glove which she held in her hand. The animal snatched the glove from her grasp, and, as he bounded backwards, fell over the carriage side. My lady uttered a scream at the sight, and I was preparing to extricate the struggling dog, when the Englishman plunged into the water. In an instant he had restored her favourite to the marchesa, and received her warmest acknowledgments. From that moment an intimacy commenced, which was destined to produce the most fatal consequences to both parties."

"Did you betray them?" I asked, somewhat impatiently.

"I was then the blind tool of the marchese. I did so," replied the old man. "I told him all particulars of the interview. He heard me in silence, but grew ashy pale with suppressed rage. Bidding me redouble my vigilance, he left me. My lady was now scarcely ever out of my sight; when one evening, a few days after what had occurred, she walked forth alone upon the garden-terrace of the villa. Her guitar was in her hand, and her favourite dog by her side. I was at a little distance, but wholly unperceived. She struck a few plaintive chords upon her instrument, and then, resting her chin upon her white and rounded arm, seemed lost in tender reverie. Would you had seen her, signor, as I beheld her then, or as one other beheld her! you would acknowledge that you had never met with her equal in beauty. Her raven hair fell in thick tresses over shoulders of dazzling whiteness and the most perfect proportion. Her deep dark eyes were thrown languidly on the ground, and her radiant features were charged with an expression of profound and pensive passion.

"In this musing attitude she continued for some minutes, when she was aroused by the gambols of her dog, who bore in his mouth a glove which he had found. As she took it from him, a letter dropped upon the floor. Had a serpent glided from its folds, it could not have startled her more. She gazed upon the paper, offended, but irresolute. Yes, she was irresolute; and you may conjecture the rest. She paused, and by that pause was lost. With a shrinking grasp she stooped to raise the letter. Her cheeks, which had grown deathly pale, again kindled with blushes as she perused it. She hesitated–cast a bewildering look towards the mansion–placed the note within her bosom–and plunged into the orange-bower."

"Her lover awaited her there?"

"He did. I saw them meet. I heard his frenzied words–his passionate entreaties. He urged her to fly–she resisted. He grew more urgent–more impassioned. She uttered a faint cry, and I stood before them. The Englishman's hand was at my throat, and his sword at my breast, with the swiftness of thought; and but for the screams of my mistress, that instant must have been my last. At her desire he relinquished his hold of me; but her cries had reached other ears, and the marchese arrived to avenge his injured honour. He paused not to inquire the nature of the offence, but, sword in hand, assailed the Englishman, bidding me remove his lady. The clash of their steel was drowned by her shrieks as I bore her away; but I knew the strife was desperate. Before I gained the house my lady had fainted; and, committing her to the charge of other attendants, I returned to the terrace. I met my master slowly walking homewards. His sword was gone–his brow was bent–he shunned my sight. I knew what had happened, and did not approach him. He sought his wife. What passed in that interview was never disclosed, but it may be guessed at from its result. That night the marchesa left her husband's halls–never to return. Next morn I visited the terrace where she had received the token. The glove was still upon the ground. I picked it up and carried it to the marchese, detailing the whole occurrence to him. He took it, and vowed as he took it that his vengeance should never rest satisfied till that glove had been steeped in her blood."

"And he kept his vow?" I asked, shuddering.

"Many months elapsed ere its accomplishment. Italian vengeance is slow, but sure. To all outward appearance, he had forgotten his faithless wife. He had even formed a friendship with her lover, which he did the more effectually to blind his ultimate designs. Meanwhile, time rolled on, and the marchesa gave birth to a child–the offspring of her seducer."

"Great God!" I exclaimed, "was that child a boy?"

"It was–but listen to me. My tale draws to a close. One night, during the absence of the Englishman, by secret means we entered the palazzo where the marchesa resided. We wandered from room to room till we came to her chamber. She was sleeping, with her infant by her side. The sight maddened the marchese. He would have stricken the child, but I held back his hand. He relented. He bade me make fast the door. He approached the bed. I heard a rustle–a scream. A white figure sprang from out the couch. In an instant the light was extinguished–there was a blow–another–and all was over. I threw open the door. The marchese came forth, The corridor in which we stood was flooded with moonlight. A glove was in his hand–it was dripping with blood. His oath was fulfilled–his vengeance complete–no, not complete, for the Englishman yet lived."

"What became of him?" I inquired.

"Ask me not," replied the old man; "you were at the Chiesa Santa Maria Maggiore this morning. If those stones could speak, they might tell a fearful story."

"And that was the reason you did not dare to unclose your eyes within those holy precincts–a film of blood floated between you and heaven."

The old man shuddered, but replied not.

"And the child?" I asked, after a pause; "what of their wretched offspring?"

"It was conveyed to England by a friend of its dead father. If he were alive, that boy would be about your age, signor."

"Indeed!" I said; a horrible suspicion flashing across my mind.

"After the Englishman's death," continued Cristofano, "my master began to treat me with a coldness and suspicion which increased daily. I was a burden to him, and he was resolved to rid himself of me. I spared him the trouble–quitted Rome–sought the mountains of the Abruzzi–and thence wandered to the fastnesses of Calabria, and became–no matter what. Here I am, Heaven's appointed minister of vengeance. The marchese dies to-night!"

"To-night! old man," I echoed, horror-stricken. "Add not crime to crime. If he has indeed been guilty of the foul offence you have named, let him be dealt with according to the offended laws of the country. Do not pervert the purposes of justice."

"Justice!" echoed Cristofano, scornfully.

"Ay, justice. You are poor and powerless, but means may be found to aid you. I will assist the rightful course of vengeance."

"You shall assist it. I have sworn he shall die before dawn, and the hand to strike the blow shall be yours."

"Mine! never!"

"Your own life will be the penalty of your obstinacy, if you refuse; nor will your refusal save him. By the Mother of Heaven, he dies! and by your hand. You saw how he was struck by your resemblance to the young Englishman this morning in the chiesa. It is wonderful! I know not who or what you are; but to me you are an instrument of vengeance, and as such I shall use you. The blow dealt by

179

you will seem the work of retribution; and I care not if you strike twice, and make my heart your second mark."

Ere I could reply he called to his comrades, and in a few moments we were speeding across the campagna.

We arrived at a high wall: the old man conducted us to a postern-gate, which he opened. We entered a garden filled with orange-trees, the perfume of which loaded the midnight air. We heard the splash of a fountain at a distance, and the thrilling notes of a nightingale amongst some taller trees. The moon hung like a lamp over the belvedere of the proud villa. We strode along a wide terrace edged by a marble balustrade. The old man pointed to an open summer-house terminating the walk, and gave me a significant look, but he spoke not. A window thrown open admitted us to the house. We were within a hall crowded with statues, and traversed noiselessly its marble floors. Passing through several chambers, we then mounted to a corridor, and entered an apartment which formed the ante-room to another beyond it. Placing his finger upon his lips, and making a sign to his comrades, Cristofano opened a door and disappeared. There was a breathless pause for a few minutes, during which I listened intently but caught only a faint sound as of the snapping of a lock.

Presently the old man returned.

"He sleeps," he said, in a low deep tone to me; "sleeps as his victim slept–sleeps without a dream of remorse; and he shall awaken, as she awoke, to despair. Come into his chamber!"

We obeyed. The door was made fast within side.

The curtains of the couch were withdrawn, and the moonlight streamed full upon the face of the sleeper. He was hushed in profound repose. No visions seemed to haunt his peaceful slumbers. Could guilt sleep so soundly? I half doubted the old man's story.

Placing us within the shadow of the canopy, Cristofano approached the bed. A stiletto glittered in his hand. "Awake!" he cried, in a voice of thunder.

The sleeper started at the summons.

I watched his countenance. He read Cristofano's errand in his eye. But he quailed not. "Cowardly assassin!" he cried, "you have well consulted your own safety in stealing on my sleep."

"And who taught me the lesson?" fiercely interrupted the old man. "Am I the first that have stolen on midnight slumber? Gaze upon this? When and how did it acquire its dye?" And he held forth a glove, which looked blackened and stained in the moonlight.

The marchese groaned aloud.

"My cabinet broken open!" at length he exclaimed–"villain! how dared you do this? But why do I rave? I know with whom I have to deal." Uttering these words he sprung from his couch, with the intention of grappling with the old man; but Cristofano retreated, and at that instant the brigands, who rushed to his aid, thrust me forward. I was face to face with the marchese.

The apparition of the murdered man could not have staggered him more. His limbs were stiffened by the shock, and he remained in an attitude of freezing terror.

"Is he come for vengeance?" he ejaculated.

"He is!" cried Cristofano. "Give him the weapon!" And a stiletto was thrust into my hand. But I heeded not the steel. I tore open my bosom–a small diamond cross was within the folds.

"Do you recollect this?" I demanded of the marchese.

"It was my wife's!" he shrieked, in amazement.

"It was upon the infant's bosom as he slept by her side on that fatal night," said Cristofano. "I saw it sparkle there."

"That infant was myself–that wife my mother!" I cried.

"The murderer stands before you! Strike!" exclaimed Cristofano.

I raised the dagger. The marchese stirred not. I could not strike.

"Do you hesitate?" angrily exclaimed Cristofano.

"He has not the courage," returned the younger Calabrian. "You reproached me this morning with want of filial duty. Behold how a son can avenge his father!"

And he plunged his stiletto within the bosom of the marchese.

"Your father is not yet avenged, young man!" cried Cristofano, in a terrible tone. "You alone can avenge him!"

Ere I could withdraw its point the old man had rushed upon the dagger which I held extended in my grasp.

He fell without a single groan.

Also from Benediction Books ...
Wandering Between Two Worlds: Essays on Faith and Art
Anita Mathias
Benediction Books, 2007
152 pages
ISBN: 0955373700

Available from www.amazon.com, www.amazon.co.uk

In these wide-ranging lyrical essays, Anita Mathias writes, in lush, lovely prose, of her naughty Catholic childhood in Jamshedpur, India; her large, eccentric family in Mangalore, a sea-coast town converted by the Portuguese in the sixteenth century; her rebellion and atheism as a teenager in her Himalayan boarding school, run by German missionary nuns, St. Mary's Convent, Nainital; and her abrupt religious conversion after which she entered Mother Teresa's convent in Calcutta as a novice. Later rich, elegant essays explore the dualities of her life as a writer, mother, and Christian in the United States– Domesticity and Art, Writing and Prayer, and the experience of being "an alien and stranger" as an immigrant in America, sensing the need for roots.

About the Author

Anita Mathias was born in India, has a B.A. and M.A. in English from Somerville College, Oxford University and an M.A. in Creative Writing from the Ohio State University. Her essays have been published in The Washington Post, The London Magazine, The Virginia Quarterly Review, Commonweal, Notre Dame Magazine, America, The Christian Century, Religion Online, The Southwest Review, Contemporary Literary Criticism, New Letters, The Journal, and two of HarperSanFrancisco's The Best Spiritual Writing anthologies. Her non-fiction has won fellowships from The National Endowment for the Arts; The Minnesota State Arts Board; The Jerome Foundation, The Vermont Studio Center; The Virginia Centre for the Creative Arts, and the First Prize for the Best General Interest Article from the Catholic Press Association of the United States and Canada. Anita has taught Creative Writing at the College of William and Mary, and now lives and writes in Oxford, England.

www.anitamathias.com,
christiancogitations.blogspot.com
wanderingbetweentwoworlds.blogspot.com

www.ingramcontent.com/pod-product-compliance
Lightning Source LLC
Chambersburg PA
CBHW050938120626
46552CB00001B/274